Just Add Magic

Just Add *Magic

Cindy Callaghan

ALADDIN MIX

New York London Toronto Sydney

ALADDIN M!X
Simon & Schuster Children's Publishing Division
1230 Avenue of the Americas, New York, NY 10020
First Aladdin M!X edition October 2010
Copyright © 2010 by Cindy Callaghan
All rights reserved, including the right of reproduction in whole or in part in any form.
ALADDIN is a trademark of Simon & Schuster, Inc., and related logo is a registered trademark of Simon & Schuster, Inc.
ALADDIN M!X and related logo are registered trademarks of Simon & Schuster, Inc.
For information about special discounts for bulk purchases, please contact Simon & Schuster Special Sales at 1-866-506-1949 or business@simonandschuster.com.
The Simon & Schuster Speakers Bureau can bring authors to your live event. For more information or to book an event contact the Simon & Schuster Speakers Bureau at 1-866-248-3049 or visit our website at www.simonspeakers.com.
Designed by Jessica Handelman
The text of this book was set in Lomba Book.
Manufactured in the United States of America/0719 OFF
11
Library of Congress Control Number 2010923139
ISBN 978-1-4424-0268-3
ISBN 978-1-4424-0269-0 (eBook)

Acknowledgments

There is nothing more magical in life than the people we share it with. I'm very lucky to be surrounded by wonderful people.

I'd like to thank my wonderful critique group, The WIPs: Chris, Gale, Shannon, Karen, Jill, Jane, Jo, Lara, and Carolee. These gals are my writing support network, and I am very fortunate to have them.

Thank you to the world's best literary agent, Sarah Davies of Greenhouse Literary Agency, who invested her time and patience in me and in Kelly's story. I am so appreciative of her and her advice. Further, I'd like to thank Julia Churchill, also of GH, for this title.

I am thankful to everyone at Aladdin M!X, most especially Alyson Heller, magical editor, who had confidence in this story from the beginning.

I've been encouraged by many friends—old, new, local, distant, college, high school, neighbors, and work. . . . Thank you all for listening to my plots, and for reading my blog . . . or for telling me you do, even if you don't (ahem . . . Julie, Chris, Pam, Tricia, and Maria.)

One word: Dad. He read draft after draft after draft.

Thanks for reminding me for the last thirty-something years that I am creative. And, Mom, thanks for giving me the 'tude that I *can* do anything! Sue and Mark, thanks for smiling and nodding through all my half-baked ideas without laughing—at least not to my face.

Thanks to my mother-in-law, who critiqued and meticulously corrected the same grammar mistakes repeatedly, and cheered on every milestone! And thanks to my dad-in-law for encouraging me through each small victory.

I need to recognize my fan club (everyone should have one), a.k.a. The Nieces. The girls who gave me more advice than I could possibly ever use in a thousand lifetimes: Anna, Mikayla, Taylor, Nikk-o-licous, Kelsey, Shawn, Lauren . . . (Sorry, Dan, John, Chris, and Sean, it's a girl thing!). And also my little fan friends from St. Mary Magdalen, some of whom inspired the characters in *Just Add Magic*—that would be you, Mel and Kylie.

The *most* magical thing in my life? My chief creative consultant, Ellie; the one-boy market research shop and marketing president, Evan; and think tank leader, Happy. These cherubs are a constant reminder of priorities in life and they've influenced every page herein.

And last but not least, my husband, Kevin, who supports me in being anything I want to be.

Just Add Magic

1

The Secret in the Attic

Question: *What do you get when you mix two girls hungry for cash with a cleaning project?*

Answer: *Kelly Quinn and Darbie O'Brien in a dark, dusty, spider-webby attic on their last day of summer vacation.*

Correction: I, Kelly Quinn, was cleaning. Darbie Rollerbladed in the clutter-free areas, careful not to bang her head on the rafters.

THUD!

I had missed Darbie this summer while she had been at her dad's house at the beach and I had been at camp. "Are you okay?" I asked.

"Fine." Darbie sat among the piles of attic stuff, rubbing her head. "Where did all this junk-arooni come from?" she asked.

"Some of it was my grandmother's. And some belongs

to the witch, Mrs. Silvers, from across the street. Her basement flooded years ago, and presto, we got her junk," I said.

"Are you gonna give it back to her?"

"She says she doesn't want any of it," I said.

Darbie lifted a heavy old book out of a tub full of old books, magazines, and newspapers. "Check out this book. It looks older than my grandpa Stan." She blew off the dust, her skin shining with sweat, and I noticed her freckles were dark from her beach tan. (I never mention her freckles out loud. Last time I did, she Rollerbladed over my sandwich: smoked ham and Muenster cheese, with honey mustard on rye.)

Books are "blah" to Darbie. I don't love them myself, unless it's my journal or one of my cookbooks.

Oh, BTW, I'm Kelly Quinn, age twelve, seventh-grader, lover of all things cooking, mediocre soccer player, average student, and best friend to Darbie O'Brien and Hannah Hernandez.

I wasn't thrilled to spend my last day of summer vacation cleaning the attic. However, I needed the money, and any time I could spend hanging with one of my BFFs couldn't be all that bad.

"Look, Kell," Darbie said excitedly, dusting off a book. "It's dated 1953." For a book to capture Darbie's attention, I figured it must've been something pretty interesting.

"Wow, that's older than my mom." I wiped the rest of the book off with the bottom of my T-shirt. "It's a *World Book Encyclopedia, Volume T.*"

"Encyclopedia? Yuck!" Darbie tossed the book like it was a hot tamale burning her fingers. I was curious, so I flipped through it. I looked for "tamale."

It only took a second for me to realize there was no tamale, tomato, turnovers, or anything else starting with the letter *T.* In fact, the book wasn't filled with anything encyclopedia-ish. The original pages were pasted over with yellowed stationery. The papers were thick, a little crunchy, and stained in places. The words on the stationery were handwritten, a little sloppy, and a few were in Spanish. I knew what I was looking at right away.

These were recipes.

I sat on the trunk and looked at each heavy page. The names of the recipes were very interesting: Forget-Me-Not Cupcakes, Love Bug Juice, and Tell Me the Truth Tea. And there were notes written all around the edges of the stationery, in the margins of the encyclopedia.

"Darbie," I said. "This isn't an encyclopedia at all. It's a bunch of recipes *hidden in* an encyclopedia. Do you know what that makes this?" I asked.

"A recipedia!" Darbie said, grabbing some chunky pearls and bejeweled sunglasses from a hatbox as she Rollerbladed by. "That sounds perfect for a Food Network junkie like you." She was right. I *love* to cook. Ever since my encounter with the famous TV chef Felice Foudini herself, I haven't been able to get enough of cooking. My mom and I cook together all the time, and my other BFF, Hannah, gave me the very first book in my cookbook collection, which consists of six books ranging across the meal, dessert, and snack spectrums. They're stored on a kitchen shelf with different colored Post-it notes sticking out from all sides.

"No, not a recipedia. Listen to this stuff: 'Induces sleep,' 'Keeps 'em quiet,' 'Brings your true *amor.*' Darbie, there's only one thing better than a cookbook, and that's a Secret Recipe Book! And that's exactly what this is."

Just then, the latch on the attic door jiggled. It rattled hard like someone was trying to break in, which was strange because I would've preferred breaking *out*. Suddenly my sweaty mom, who had been cleaning out the garage, tumbled into the attic from pushing the door so hard. She stood at the top of the stairs with a red bandana covering her hair and ears, and yellow rubber dishwashing gloves covering her hands, looking like she'd just appeared on *Extreme Makeover: Dork Edition*. Thank goodness Hannah wasn't here to see the outfit. She's our local fashionista, particularly known for always color coordinating her headband, outfit, and socks.

"Mrs. Silvers just called." Mom sounded frustrated that

Mrs. Silvers had interrupted her cleaning day. "She said Rosey pooped in her yard again. Would you please go over and pick it up?"

Mrs. Silvers is my older-than-dirt neighbor from across the street and she's as nasty as a witch. She's convinced that Rosey, our beagle, flies over, or tunnels under, our fenced-in backyard every day for the sole purpose of pooping in her yard. One day, when Rosey was a puppy, before we had the fence, she actually *did* poop in that yard and Mrs. Silvers saw her. Rosey hasn't left our yard since. Still, thanks to that incident, I scoop for every dog on Coyote Street that uses Mrs. Silvers's yard as their personal bathroom.

While scooping didn't thrill me, I was dying to get out of the hot attic to get some sunlight and fresh air. "Sure," I said, and Mom vanished back down the stairs.

Darbie said, "She looks like she's arming herself to enter a chicken pox colony."

"Unlike you, my mom hates bugs and spiders. She won't touch them. When she cleans, she's afraid they'll land in her hair or crawl into her ears," I explained.

Darbie considered this. I could tell she was thinking about the bug thing.

"Before you ask, no. You can't stay and catch any. Besides, bats and rats hang out in attics, not bugs," I told her.

When our attic work was pretty much done, we headed

across the street to Mrs. Silvers's house. I walked, pooper-scooper in hand, while Darbie Rollerbladed. She blades pretty much everywhere. The crazy thing is that Darbie isn't a great blader. She's an okay blader who just manages to keep herself upright. (Of course, I don't tell her that.) She stumbled to the driveway, to the sidewalk, to the street, to the grass. I held out my arm in case she needed it for balance.

I couldn't get the Secret Recipe Book out of my mind. "Why do you think they're hidden in the encyclopedia?"

"What? The recipes?" Darbie asked.

"Darb, not just any recipes, *secret recipes*."

"Right. Well, they are probably hidden because they're secret."

"Exactly what I was thinking." As we got to the yard I warned Darbie, "Don't look directly into Mrs. Silvers's eyes. You'll turn to stone."

Mrs. Silvers yelled from her front porch, "If I see that mutt again, I'm going to call the pound!" She was surprisingly loud for a woman who looked old enough to be dead. Besides the flabby wrinkles that hung from a face covered in a perpetual scowl, her white hair made her recognizable from miles away. It was short and somehow able to defy gravity by sticking straight up in the air. It reminded me of one of those toy trolls that sits on top of a pencil. And while I assumed she had feet, we couldn't see them under the weird muumuu/housedress thing she always wore.

"Man, Silvers is a grouch-a-saurus," Darbie said under her breath.

"You would be too if you were a hundred years old and bent over all crooked," I said. I didn't actually know how old she was, but a hundred sounded about right.

"Why do you have to scoop the poop?" Darbie asked.

"Since Rosey's mostly my dog, I have to be responsible for her." I mimicked my dad on "responsible for her." "And because, if I don't, I won't get my allowance, which I need to support my Swirley habit." Darbie nodded understandingly. She and Hannah had the habit too.

Super Swirleys were the best milkshakes in Delaware, and possibly the world. They're ice cream and all kinds of other stuff blended into a heavenly frozen concoction. I can't live without them. They were made at Sam's Super iScream, which, luckily, was within walking distance from my house.

After a refreshing breath of mid-Atlantic air, we headed back across the street and entered my house through the garage. We stopped in the kitchen for ice water.

Our vegetable-themed kitchen was my favorite room in the house. The walls were painted artichoke green. Our plates were eggplant purple and stacked nicely in a tall glass-doored cabinet. The wallpaper border was a conga line of dancing carrots, cucumbers, bell peppers, radishes, and mushrooms, all with legs, holding pretty much every kitchen appliance, gadget, and accessory imaginable.

Mom appeared, thankfully sans her protective gear. Her spider-free blond hair was flipped up in a clip. She'd changed into a clean LIFE IS GOOD shirt, gray cotton mini-skirt, and cute sandals: undorked. "If I pretend Darbie isn't wearing Rollerblades in my kitchen, will you girls load all the attic stuff into the minivan?" she asked.

We kept quiet, not excited about loading.

"After that, maybe we'll get you two busy bees a soda."

Silence. *No sale,* as my dad would say.

"Oh, all right. After we drop off all the attic stuff at Goodwill, I'll pay you for your work and treat you to Swirley's." We smiled.

Darbie asked Mom, "Can we maybe meet Hannah-Hoobi-Haha at the pool after her laps?" Darbie loved to add a little jazz to Hannah's name.

Mom said, "I think we can do that."

SOLD to the lady with the minivan!

Darbie and I looked at each other and did our happy dance by swiveling our hips in a small circle and shifting our bodies from side to side. We sang, "Oh yeah. It's your birthday, it's my birthday."

Darbie switched to flip-flops and we loaded the van. I worked quickly because I was anxious to fill my belly with a Super Swirley and read the Secret Recipe Book. When we were done, I stuck the book in a canvas messenger bag that I wore across my chest.

As luck would have it, my little brother, Buddy, tagged along. He was five going on annoying. The only thing good about having Buddy with us was that he couldn't be rummaging through my bedroom and smearing his boogers on the wall. (Seriously, I actually caught him doing it.) Before we were even out of the driveway he was singing "The Wheels on the Bus" painfully loud. Darbie and I put our hands over our ears. As we drove off in the noise-polluted, air-conditioned van, I saw Mrs. Silvers looking out her living room window.

Buddy sang, "ALL THROUGH THE TOWN!"

2

A Mysterious Warning

Soon after pulling out of the driveway, I saw a familiar, tall, skinny, long-haired figure wearing a loose bathing suit cover-up and dripping with water as she walked down the street. It was Hannah Hernandez, the third of our BFF trio. Like Darbie, she lives in my neighborhood. We all met each other on the first day of kindergarten, when we sat together on the school bus in terrified silence. We've been best pals ever since.

Darbie hung her head out the window. "Hey there, Hannah-Heidi-HoHoHo. Done swimming?"

She nodded and got into the van, careful to sit on her towel. "Done for the season. I'm gonna miss it."

"We're heading somewhere that'll cheer you up," I said.

"Sam's?" she asked. We nodded. "Awesome! A Swirley is exactly what I need right now."

The minivan pulled into the strip shopping mall, which had three stores: Sam's, Cup O' Joe (my mom goes there a lot for coffee), and La Cocina. La Cocina was a Mexican cooking store, but they have some other stuff too, like Mexican clothes, candles, and homemade arts and crafts. I walked past it all the time, but I'd never actually been inside—our regular supermarket had everything I needed. Also, for some unexplained reason, the place gave me the willies.

Maybe because the windows were so heavily tinted that all you could see when you looked at them was your reflection. I saw my mirror image standing between Hannah and Darbie. I was shorter than Hannah, but not as short as Darbie. My hair was light brown, wavy, and touched my shoulders, while Hannah's was light, straight, and long (like her mom's), and Darbie's was dark brown, short, and sort of mussed-up.

I have big, dark, chestnut brown eyes that people always complimented. One front tooth slants so that it slightly crosses the other. The orthodontist promised she could fix it, but sometimes I wasn't sure I wanted it fixed.

My skin was smooth and naturally tan—in the summer

it gets pretty dark. Sometimes I'd study my face and body in the mirror, and I know a lot of girls don't say this about themselves, but I liked what I saw. I wasn't joining the pageant circuit, but there was nothing I looked at and said 'I hate it.'

The front door of La Cocina is regular glass, so I could see inside. It was dingy and dark.

Bud continued to sing, and literally *marched* into Sam's.

"He is totally embarrassing," Darbie said.

I said, "Welcome to my world of *Life with Bud*."

My mom tried to be patient with him. She got him ice cream and a minute later said, "You girls can walk home, right?"

I nodded. She handed Darbie and me envelopes with our pay (Thirty-two big ones! EACH!), and an extra ten-dollar bill to cover the Swirleys. Then she took Buddy by the hand and marched him right out the door and back into the van.

"Thank goodness," Hannah said. "He was giving me a headache."

Sam, the owner, said, "Hi girls. You know, Kelly, I'm thinking of taking Darbie's advice and naming a grape Swirley after you: The Peanut Butter and Kelly Jelly."

"Really? That would be great. Do you want my picture?" I asked. "You can put it right here next to your postcard collection." I pointed to the cards he kept under the glass at the counter.

"I don't think that will be necessary," he said.

I glanced at the postcard collection, noticing one I hadn't seen before. "Where's this one from?" I asked.

"Oh, I love that one. A friend sent it to me from Mexico." He wiped the counter with a towel. "Now, what can I get for you?"

Darbie got a Rocket Launching Rainbow because it had, like, every flavor and every topping. I got a Black and White. (That's vanilla and chocolate ice cream with chocolate syrup.)

"Let me guess," Sam said to Hannah. "Bowl Me Over Chocolate Brownie with extra fudge, and Snickers." Hannah smiled.

We got a table. I took my messenger bag off my chest and slid out the big book.

Hannah asked, "What's that?"

I filled her in. "We found this when we were cleaning out my attic. On the outside it looks like an ordinary 1953 *World Book Encyclopedia, Volume T.* But on the inside . . ." I opened the book. "The encyclopedia pages have been pasted over with old stationery containing handwritten recipes. The recipes are *hidden* inside the encyclopedia. You know what that makes this?"

Hannah looked at the book. "A recipedia?"

"Exact-a-mundo," Darbie said.

Sam delivered the shakes and we thanked him. I

dipped a long spoon into mine and savored the blend.

"No. Look at the unusual names of these recipes. And look at these notes. It's a Secret Recipe Book," I said.

Hannah nodded in agreement. She wasn't as enthusiastic as I'd hoped. "Sure, okay," she said.

I turned each page slowly and carefully, so Hannah could read them. I thought that if she saw the papers herself, she'd understand how totally cool this was.

Hannah pointed to the top of one page. "It's faded, but do you see this logo? I think it's from the Wilmington Library."

Hannah knew the logo because she studied there a lot. If my favorite place was the kitchen, then Hannah's was the library.

Hannah turned all the pages to look at the inside back cover. "Look at this stamp—*WL*. That's definitely the Wilmington Library's stamp."

"So?" Darbie asked.

"So, at one time this encyclopedia belonged to the Wilmington Library. I'm guessing before it was a recipedia," Hannah said as she stirred together all the chocolate elements in her Swirley.

"Not recipedia, Secret Recipe Book," I said. "You know what I'm thinking?"

Darbie and Hannah shrugged.

"I'm thinking this is the perfect time for me to start a cooking club," I said. I had wanted to start one ever since my mom and I went to watch a live Cooking Network show starring a chef named Felice Foudini. Of everyone in the studio, she chose to bring *me* up on stage to taste her chili. Well, I knew a *lot* about chili because every year my mom and I enter the Alfred Nobel School Chili Cook-Off.

So when Felice Foudini asked me if I liked her chili, I told her that I thought the cayenne pepper overpowered the cumin. She was shocked that a kid knew so much about spices. Everyone clapped for me, and at that moment I knew my future would be about cooking.

Right around the time of the Felice Foudini show, my mom said I could start a club when I was in seventh grade. She probably thought I'd forgotten, but no.

BTW, seventh grade was starting TOMORROW!

Hannah said, "It's about time you started that club. You've talked about it for long enough."

I ripped a blank sheet of paper out of the spiral notebook that was in my messenger bag.

"Let's start tomorrow," I said, "with something from this book. It looks like we'll need some ingredients. There are a few in here that I've never heard of."

"You?" Darbie asked. "If you've never heard of them, then maybe they don't exist."

Hannah was still reading over my shoulder. She pointed to the word *amor*. "That's Spanish. It means 'love.'" She pointed to another word. "That's Spanish too, it means 'mix.' This word here, that's 'bread.'" Hannah was practically fluent in Spanish. She was born in Barcelona, where her mother met her father. They lived there for a few years before coming to live in Delaware. At her house they speak Spanish and English.

Darbie said, "Maybe it's a *Mexican* recipedia."

Why couldn't she call it a Secret Recipe Book? "Maybe," I said. "But there are recipes that definitely aren't Mexican, like these cupcakes. Anyway, you've given me an idea for where we can find the ingredients we need."

Strings of shells hung from the doorknob of La Cocina. They knocked together as the door inched closed behind us, cutting us off from the scent of Cup O' Joe's and the rest of Wilmington. A big stuffed bear welcomed us into an alternate universe. The bright sunlight was blocked by the tinted windows. It took a minute before the spots in front of my eyes went away. I didn't know if it was the effect of the icy Swirley in my hand, or the coolness in the room, but I felt a frigid whisper on the back of my knees.

Quietly I asked Darbie and Hannah, "Do you have the feeling you're being watched?" The words made me shiver.

Darbie followed the worn braided rug around the store and studied the animal heads mounted on the orange paint-chipped walls. "Maybe that's because we *are* being watched," she said, pointing to a moose staring at us with shiny glass eyes. "Creeeeepy." She crinkled her nose.

I scanned the shelves of spices. There were hundreds of little bottles. The ones pushed to the front seemed new. I could see they were filled with powders, elixirs, extracts, and syrups. Other little golden and greenish jars and vials capped with corks were pushed to the back. For some bottles, the glass was so thick I could hardly see through it. On the bottom of each container was a small handwritten label containing the item's name and a price. I lifted several, and noticed they were organized alphabetically. I chose six items I needed. They were all from the back of the shelves. I gave them to Hannah and Darbie to hold.

On the next set of shelves there were rows of see-through plastic bags of various sizes filled with all kinds of leaves, berries, stems, roots, and stalks. A maroon, star-shaped tag with a name and price dangled from each. I studied my list and took the bag I needed.

A voice startled us. "*Hola, niñas.*" A woman had materialized.

Hannah offered, "*Hola, Señora—*"

"Perez, Señora Perez," she said. Señora Perez was small—shorter than Darbie, who was the third-shortest kid in our grade. She had black hair streaked with gray and piled high on top of her head like a moldy pineapple.

There was an awkward pause during which Señora Perez looked us each up and down, starting with the freckles on Darbie's legs, up to Hannah's wet hair, and landing on my brown eyes.

"Ah." She studied my face. "You are the daughter of Señora Becky Quinn." She gave Darbie one more quick check from head to toe. "And you must be the one that roller-skates."

We nodded. This woman was good.

"You are buying those?" She stared at the stuff we cradled.

"*Si*," I said, impressed with my Spanish.

Señora Perez waddled on her short legs around the counter. She fumbled with the chain around her neck until it rescued a pair of reading glasses from her many scarves. She rang us up, pressing down hard on the old metal cash register keys. As she did, she peered over the top of her glasses suspiciously, like a detective might during an interrogation.

She continued to stare as she put our purchases in a brown paper bag, careful to cushion the bottles with tissue paper. I paid her with my attic cleaning money.

Finally Señora Perez spoke. "Would you like me to read your palm?" Then, looking at Hannah, she said, "You do not believe in palm readings." Hannah held a straight face—*a poker face*, as my dad says.

Señora Perez wiped her hands on the apron fastened around her midsection and motioned for me to sit down on a stool. She inhaled deeply through her nose, forcing her nostrils open wide, and reached for my hand. The room was quiet. She gently dragged her long nails across my palm. Darbie sucked so hard on her Swirley that she reached the bottom and made a loud *slurp!* The sound vibrated off the walls. Señora Perez didn't seem to notice. Her head tilted down until her chin was buried in the extra skin around her neck and she studied my hand. "Ah . . ."

Darbie looked over Señora's shoulder at my hand.

"*Si, si.* I see, *niña* . . ." Señora Perez squinted at my palm.

"See what? See what?" Darbie asked.

She said, "I see a book."

I felt imaginary snakes crawl up the back of my shirt.

Señora Perez took her reading glasses off and shuffled toward a hallway at the back of the store. Instead of a door, long strands of brightly colored beads hung from the ceiling to the floor. Before passing through, she turned and said, "Beware: *Quien siembra vientos recoge temtestades.*"

Then she disappeared into the beads.

3

Another Warning

Question: *What is the probability of
getting two eerie warnings in fifteen minutes?*

Answer (using no math at all): *Zero probability . . . probably.*

was shocked, amazed, and totally freaked out at the
same time, if that's possible. Darbie sat on the curb in
front of La Cocina and changed out of her flip-flops and
back into her Rollerblades. We headed down Main Street
toward my house. The only sound was the *swoosh-swoosh* of
Darbie's blades on the cement and an occasional passing car.

"That was whacked out," Darbie finally said.

"How could she have known about the Book?" I asked.

Hannah said, "She said she saw *a* book, not *the* Book.
She could have meant any book. Besides, don't get too
excited, that palm reading stuff isn't true."

"Don't get too excited? On the very day I find an ancient book of hidden secret recipes, a bizarre fortune-teller looks into my hand and sees a book. As in, a book that will change my future, maybe the course of my entire life. *That's* very exciting."

"Now it's an *ancient* book of secret recipes? Come on, Kell," Hannah said. "It's some papers glued into an encyclopedia. It's not like you discovered Santa's Naughty and Nice List."

Darbie mimicked Señora Perez with mock exaggeration, "And what about BEEEEWAAARRRREEE, MooHaHaHah!" She rubbed her palms together like an evil scientist.

I didn't see the humor in a fortune-teller giving a warning. "Yeah. What was with that? What does it mean?"

Hannah said, "I can't translate it exactly, but it's something like 'you get what you deserve.'"

"You get what you deserve," I repeated thoughtfully. "What do we deserve?"

"What's this 'we' business?" Darbie said. "Don't bring me into this. You get a corny warning from some kooky Mexican fortune-teller, it's yours. It's all yours, Kelly Quinn."

Hannah said, "Get a grip. Like Darbie said, it was just a weird comment from some senile old lady. Don't let it get to you."

As I walked, I dug the Book out of my messenger bag and opened the front cover. A scrap of paper blew out. I tried to grab it, but the wind swept it out of my fingertips. "Get that! It's from the Book."

Darbie picked up the pace of her swooshing and snatched the paper before it dipped into a storm drain.

Hannah and I caught up to her. "Good catch. What does it say?" I asked.

"It's tough to tell because the ink is pretty faded," Darbie said. "Something like, 'Remember to Beware of the Law of Re . . . Re . . .' I think it says 'Rewind.'"

"What the heck does that mean?" I thought out loud, "Rewind . . ."

Darbie smirked. "What the heck does that mean? Rewind. What the heck does that mean? Rewind. What the heck does—"

"I get it. You're funny. But, seriously, let me see that." I examined the note. "It doesn't say rewind, it says returns. It's 'Remember to Beware of the Law of Returns.'"

Darbie said, "Well, that's just terrific. You know I've gone my entire life without ever getting an eerie warning, and now we get two in fifteen minutes. What are the chances of that?"

4

My Cooking Club

Ingredients:
3 twelve-year-old girls
2 eerie warnings
1 ancient book of secret recipes
7 new spices from La Cocina

Directions:
Mix together to create an extraordinary type of club.

I jumped high on my bed. On the first jump I slid the ceiling tile out of place. On the second I got my journal. On the third jump I slid the tile back into place.

My journal was a superfat pink composition notebook. I've written in it for years—things like lists of my favorite Christmas presents, what I wanted to be when I grow up, names for future pets, and things I wanted to be sure to remember. But I had never written a warning until now.

Warnings:

Beware:

1. Quien siembra vientos recoge temtestades.
(Translation)
Beware:
You get what you deserve.

2. Remember to Beware of the Law of Returns

I also wrote about special memories in here. I've read the page about meeting Felice Foudini a hundred times. I turned to the page about the cooking club and made an important update of my plan.

It was time to do the final round of nagging about starting my cooking club.

With journal in hand, I was lured to the kitchen by the smell of roasting garlic. Mom was singing the jazz song, "With a Wink and a Smile." She thought she sang well, but . . . let's just say that the truth was written in my journal.

"Is that your favorite song? You know you sing great." I buttered her up. "Whatcha making? It smells really good."

"Chili, what else? The contest is in a week. Are you in?"

"You bet," I said. The annual Alfred Nobel School Chili Cook-Off is a major big deal in our town. Everyone who likes to cook enters with their own special recipe. The Cook-Off is held at Alfred Nobel School the first weekend after school starts. All the kids attend in their sports uniforms: the soccer team, cheerleading squad, football team, bowling team . . . I wondered why we didn't have a cooking team and made a quick note in my journal. The winner is named Wilmington's Chili King or Queen and gets to wear the cherished chili pepper necklace and matching crown.

Mrs. Rusamano, Frankie and Tony Rusamano's mom, is the reigning four-year champion. Last year, Mrs. R. wore the chili necklace to back-to-school night, and to the Alfred Nobel School Halloween and Christmas socials. (I think this made my mom a little jealous.) Mrs. R. is an amazing Italian cook, and she also makes really good chili that the contest judge, our principal, Mr. James G. Avery, loves.

Mom continued, "I heard there's a new judge, some fancy schmancy new teacher at your school."

Mr. Avery isn't judging this year? "Mom, that changes *everything*," I said.

"I know! We've got to get to work. I made a schedule for the week so we can prepare."

"Cool. I have a good feeling about this year, Mom. We're going to smash Mrs. R. like a clove of garlic." I punched my fist on the kitchen counter for emphasis.

She stopped chopping a green pepper and looked at me with narrowed eyes and a tilted head. "You know, Kelly Quinn, I can always tell when you want something."

"That's because you're the smartest person in Delaware, possibly the whole world."

She smiled. "That's probably true. But did you know that I can tell fortunes?" She scooted a slice of pepper across the counter for me.

"Oh, really?"

"Of course. I can see into the unknown, the beyond."

"No you can't." I crunched on the pepper.

"Well, let's just give it a try and we'll see." My mom wiped her hands on a napkin and got a big green honeydew melon from the refrigerator. She took a clean dish towel out of a drawer and hung it over her head. She rubbed her hands all over the honeydew like it was a crystal ball. She thought she was so funny. I rolled my eyes.

"Oh, lovely green melon that shows me things that I can't see. Show me Kelly's bedroom floor." She studied the melon. "I see it! It's covered with dirty socks, a wet towel, and M&M's wrappers. Can that be right, green melon? That must be another girl's bedroom. Please check again." She gazed at the fruit. "Nope. Same dirty bedroom floor. Thank you, green melon." Mom said, "So, you didn't clean your room, but you've written in that pink journal of yours."

"You're right, Mom. You *are* an amazing fortune-teller." My dad had taught me that the first rule of selling is to find out what someone *needs*. And he's a salesman, so he knows what he's talking about. "You must get tired from working so hard to make nice dinners for us," I said. "Wouldn't it be nice for someone to cook for *you*?"

"Okay, tell me what you're cooking up, Kelly Quinn." Mom took a teacup out of a cabinet and a mesh metal tea ball off a hook.

I showed Mom the page in my pink journal with the change I'd just made:

SECRET Cooking Club
Members: Kelly Quinn, Darbie O'Brien, Hannah Hernandez
Place and time: Kelly Quinn's kitchen, 3:15 p.m.

"Why is it secret?"

Oops. I should've made that update *after* showing Mom, but I thought fast. "Because, it's more fun that way."

"So, Darbie and Hannah are going to come over and cook in my kitchen?" She sprinkled different colored tea leaves into the open mesh ball, snapped it shut, and dangled it into her mug by a slim silver chain.

I nodded with a smile.

She didn't seem as excited as I was. "What about homework?"

I had expected this question. "We can do some of it here together, and I'll do the rest when they go home."

"Soccer?" she asked as the kettle whistled.

"*If* I make the team, we would cook on days off, or after practice."

"And who will you be cooking *for*?" she asked as she blew on her tea.

I had expected this question too. "You and Daddy."

"Who else?" she asked.

"That's it. Just you and Daddy. And if you wear a dish towel on your head, it'll just be Daddy." She gave me her patented "annoyed mom" look. "I was thinking Buddy could go next door to the Barneys,'" I said, referring to Charlotte Barney, the meanest seventh-grade girl, who just happened to live next door. She thought Bud was the most irritating creature under the sun. (She wasn't entirely wrong.)

"No. He'll be here. And you and your friends have to be nice to him."

"But MOomm, he'll ruin everything. You know how he is."

"I'll talk to him about not ruining everything."

I made a pouty face. "Oh, all right." I hopped off the kitchen stool and dashed to the phone to call the girls.

"Hold it right there, Kelly Quinn," Mom called to me. "Can you name that tune in two notes?"

She looked at me, waiting for me to guess what two-syllable word she was thinking about. "Clean-up," she finally said, because I didn't know the word she was thinking of.

My mom is a freak show about messes. She's always

like, "Make the bed, pick up your shoes, put your clothes away, don't write on the walls, blah, blah, blah."

I said, "We'll load the dishwasher. And I'll put the big pots in the sink to soak."

"And do you think the dishwasher will just empty itself?" she asked.

I can name that tune in two notes: Clean Freak.

"I'll tell you what," she said. "If you run the dishwasher and do a good job cleaning up everything else, I'll help you empty it before you go to bed."

Sold to the lady with the green melon!

Mom wiped her hands and stuck one out so we could shake on it. "I'm going to be here keeping an eye on you girls." She pointed to her eyes and pointed to me. "Now, go upstairs and clean your room. Then you can send an e-mail to the girls and invite them to your cooking club. Oh, sorry, *secret* cooking club. Don't worry, I won't tell a soul. But I can tell Dad, right? He's one of the sharpest tacks in the box, and he might notice if three girls are here cooking in our kitchen."

"Okay, but that's it," I said.

Mom said, "Oh, one more thing. Mrs. Silvers gave me some fresh-picked apples today. Please pack one for lunch tomorrow and don't throw it out."

From Mrs. Silvers? Did you check it for poison? "Okay," I said.

I worked my way back up to my bedroom. I tidied up a bit, and emailed the girls. I put the journal back into the ceiling tiles, slid the Secret Recipe Book under my bed, and wiggled into my bed. And, three, two, one, pounce! Rosey jumped onto the bed and burrowed herself under my covers. (I don't know if all beagles sleep under the covers, but mine does.) She kept my legs really warm in the winter, with the exception of the occasional rub from a cold, wet nose. It didn't take long before she was asleep and snoring. I was right behind her.

5

The Wonderful World of Seventh Grade

Question: *How many times does a girl have
her first day of seventh grade?*

Answer: *Once.*

So, it should've been a wonderful and memorable morning, right? Oh, it started out okay. I dressed in my new deep-cuffed denim capris and made myself an awesome gourmet lunch with an alphabet theme: Avocado, Bacon, and Chicken sandwich, with Dill. That's when my mom looked out the window. I can name who she saw in four notes: Char-lotte Bar-ney.

"Kell, there goes Charlotte. If you hurry, you can walk to the bus stop with her."

I rolled my eyes. "That's okay. I'm going to walk to the other bus stop."

"Don't be silly. That's farther." And that's when she did it. She yelled out the window. "Good morning, Charlotte. Wait up, Kelly will be right there."

Mom and I need to have a serious chat later. What she can't seem to remember (ever), is that Charlotte Barney might be my next door neighbor, but she is also my archenemy. (BTW, having an archenemy isn't as glamorous as it sounds.)

I left the house and slammed the door behind me so that my mom would know I was mad and walked with Charlotte, whose outfit made me think twice about my favorite deep-cuffed denim capris.

She wore a supershort plaid miniskirt that I knew was from Abercrombie & Fitch, a matching T-shirt, and a loose dangly belt. Her hair bounced with fresh blond curls, and I think I smelled perfume. Charlotte talked about her summer and being in her cousin's wedding, wearing a dress "with organza roses at the hem."

All I heard was, *Blah, blah, blah.*

". . . soccer tryouts . . ."

Blah, blah.

"My father told the real estate developer . . ."

BLAH!

We boarded the bus and she "blah-ed" to me as if I didn't already know she was awful, as if I had somehow suffered a major brain-fart causing me to forget the peak of her evilness, what she did to my ninth birthday party—which was supposed to be a surprise party. She got mad at me for something stupid (I don't even remember what), so she told me that my surprise birthday party was the next day. *What kind of person would do that?*

She was still jabbering when Hannah and Darbie got on at the next stop. They sat on either side of me in the very back seat. Misty sat with Charlotte a few seats in front of us, and it was as if I had never been there.

Normally, Hannah was color coordinated: purple pants and socks, purple clip in her hair (always a matching clip in her hair), and a matching striped shirt. But apparently she had changed her style for seventh grade.

Her hair was down. It had grown very long and blond over the summer. And it looked like it had been straightened or shined. She wore skinny jeans that showed off her long legs, which had grown longer and skinnier. But what I noticed most was her shirt. Big white letters spelled LUCKYBRAND. Hannah had gone from fashionable to majorly trendy.

I diverted my stare from Hannah's outfit and stacked our backpacks up on the seat in front of us.

I whispered, "My mom says we can meet at my house, starting today." Darbie gave me a fist bump. Hannah smiled, but I sensed she was more interested in the Rusamano boys who were getting on the bus, because she was looking at them, not us.

There was a universal, "Frankkkayayayayay!" from the boys. Frankie high-fived everyone he passed. He and his brother Tony sat with the boys in the middle of the bus.

Soon, the bus chatter spilled out the double doors, into school, past the trophy case, and to the lockers. We had each brought in stuff to decorate our lockers. Hannah had pictures of that hot guy from the biggest summer movie hit, *Vampire High*, Darbie had clipped magazine pictures of extreme sports, and I'd brought an autographed picture of Felice Foudini that I'd gotten when I joined her fan club.

I entered the Home Ec room. It didn't take a fortune-teller to predict that Home Ec was going to be my favorite class.

I sat in the front row. The new teacher, Mr. Douglass, walked in a few minutes late. I suspected that he could be the only person, besides Felice Foudini, who loved cooking as much as me.

"Goooood morning"—he paused for dramatic effect— "future chefs of America!" Mr. Douglass used his arms when he talked. "It's a glorious day in seventh-grade Home Economics." He sat on his desk, his long legs reaching the floor. "As you know, this is the first time this class is being offered at Alfred Nobel School. What you might not know is that this is a trial program, and I really want to make it a huge success." He wrote the words "huge success" on the board. I wrote them in my Home Ec notebook.

"Let's create something deeee-licious. Today, and for the next two weeks, is Free Expression. That means we won't have any set structure. Use the tools and ingredients at your stations to make whatever you're inspired to create. Class, cook with your heart"—he closed his eyes and clenched his fists—"and your soul." When he opened his eyes, they sparkled. "Begin."

I raced to one of the six kitchen areas set up around the large, bright room and claimed my space. I looked at the various recipe cards scattered on the countertop and opened the pantry to see what I had to work with. I felt inspired to make supermoist butter cupcakes with buttercream frosting.

I started at the top of the recipe card and added all the basic dry ingredients to a bowl. As I sifted two cups of all-purpose flour, I noticed the Home Ec room had grown unruly with raised hands. Kids surrounded Mr. Douglass and tried to be louder than one another so that he could hear *their* questions:

"What does T-B-S-P mean?"

"Which bowl should we use?"

"How do you use this mixer-thing?"

I cracked an egg and whipped it up with butter, amused by the frenzy surrounding me. Once I blended the wet and dry ingredients, I dipped my finger in to taste. It was okay, but not great. I liked my batter to be GREAT. Felice

Foudini says you won't have *awesome* cupcakes, cake, or muffins without totally awesome batter first.

I decided to stray from the recipe on the card. I went to the pantry at the head of the classroom to see what I could find. Instant vanilla pudding. That was good, but not enough. I passed the mob surrounding Mr. Douglass and opened the double doors of the refrigerator. Sliding some stuff around, I saw the thing that would add the zest I was looking for: cream cheese.

I popped the cream cheese into the microwave to soften it a bit before adding it to my ingredients. With the hand mixer, I blended it into the batter. Then I added the pudding mix. I was so busy blending my batter while slowly turning the bowl that I didn't notice the room get quiet. When I looked up I saw Mr. Douglass with a strange look on his face and I thought he was mad because I had done something I wasn't supposed to.

I turned off the mixer.

He picked up the recipe card and looked on the countertop and in the trash area. He scrutinized the empty pudding box and the empty cream cheese container. "I'm sorry," I said. "Were you saving those for something?"

The expression on his face slowly eased itself into a smile. "No, not at all." He dunked a spoon into my batter and tasted it. "This is delicious, Miss Quinn. You are quite the independent chef who is not afraid to experiment and explore your creativity." He clapped—slow, deep claps with his hands cupped. "Perhaps I can put this into the oven for you. Then you could start over from the top and give the class a bit of a demonstration. That will allow me to address the questions of many students."

Actually, I wasn't thrilled to let go of the fab batter. And I wasn't excited to disclose the ingredients I had added to make the batter so fabulous in the first place, either.

"Of course. I would love to," I said.

6

Lunch

Mix together:
1 secret
1 tableful of seventh-grade hotties
2 Rusamano boys
1 evil neighbor who's out to get me
2 packages of Twinkies
A splash of yellow mustard

Directions:
Pack all ingredients in a school cafeteria and
wait patiently for it to boil over.

In a lot of ways, the Alfred Nobel cafeteria was like an
indoor soccer field.

The ceiling was high, the walls cement. And no
matter what color you painted them, or how many posters
you hung, they would still be cold, hard, cement. Sound
vibrates off the walls and ceiling, much like at an indoor

soccer field. Even if no one was talking (which never happened), the clatter of forks, plates stacking and clanking, and the cash register dinging fill the large room with sound. It was so noisy that sometimes you need to talk very loudly to be heard.

There weren't referees, but there were lunch monitors (sort of the same thing). The monitors kept order and prevented food fights, drawing on the tables, and running around. They sent troublemakers to Mr. Avery's office. (Darbie and Mr. Avery have spent a lot of time together over the years.)

Picking a good lunch table on the first day of school was critical, because whatever table I picked could be our table for the rest of the year. Hannah conferred with me. "You're getting the table against the wall, right?"

"Right." I rushed there to save seats while Hannah and Darbie got in line to buy their lunches. I never buy cafeteria food. I always pack my own lunch.

I spread out a red-and-white gingham dish towel like a place mat, took out my ABCD sandwich, a bottle of water, and a homemade brownie. (I used walnuts, pecans, and hazelnuts. My dad says they're *the best brownies this side of the Mason-Dixon line*.) Lastly, I took out the apple that came from Mrs. Silvers. Hesitantly, I bit into it. It was superjuicy, snow white inside, and incredibly sweet. It may have been the best I'd ever eaten.

Hannah arrived at our table with her tray containing a banana, yogurt, and soft pretzel with a packet of yellow mustard. I looked at her tray and held up the mustard. "You don't have to give up taste to be healthy," I said.

"What do you mean?" Hannah asked.

I went to the condiment table, took a little paper cup, and squeezed some extrahot brown mustard and honey into it. I stirred and tasted with my pinkie finger. *Perfecto.*

"Try this."

She broke off a little piece of pretzel, dipped, and tasted. "Oh, this is so good. Thanks."

I shrugged. "Anytime."

"Look over there." Hannah indicated a table of seventh-grade boys. "Frankie got so tan this summer. He's even cuter than last year." She reached into the pocket of her jeans and took out a glittery grape lip gloss and rolled it across her lips. The glitter and shine looked good. Maybe I should consider lip gloss this year.

"Frankie Rusamano, cute?" Darbie asked. She tilted her head and looked at the boys' table. "All I think about when I look at Frankie and Tony is how they cried and cried on the first day of kindergarten. Remember? They wouldn't let go of Mrs. R. and get on the bus? She had to drive them to school and they both had a meltdown when she finally peeled them off her and left."

Frankie and Tony Rusamano lived in my neighborhood, but a few streets farther away than Hannah and Darbie. Our moms all knew one another.

I studied Frankie Rusamano and his fraternal twin, Tony. Even though they were twins, Frankie and Tony were as different as Hannah and Darbie. Frankie was the leader of the seventh-grade boys. Everyone wanted to be his friend. "I don't know, Darb. Maybe it's time to forget about the crying and look at the Rusamano boys differently," I said.

"Boys? With an *s*? I was only talking about one boy—Frankie. Do you think Tony's cute?" Hannah asked.

That wasn't an easy question to answer. Tony was hard to figure out. Frankie's looks and personality were obvious. "I can't really tell. His hair covers a lot of his face, and his clothes are so baggy, I'm not sure what's underneath." Tony hunched over a heaping plate of greasy French fries swimming in ketchup. As he ate the top layer, he added more ketchup.

"You think Tony Rusamano is cute!" Darbie said incredibly loudly.

Immediately I averted my gaze from the boys' table to my apple. "O M G!" I exclaimed, hopeful that a swig of water would wash the hot red off my face. "That was so loud." Thank goodness the cafeteria was noisy, or most of Alfred Nobel School would have heard her.

Darbie slapped a hand over her mouth and darted her eyes around the room. "No one's looking."

Hannah surveyed the cafeteria. "I think it's okay."

I pointed my fork at Darbie. "You got lucky, O'Brien." I exhaled. That was close. I didn't reopen the subject, but I silently considered Tony's cuteness. I watched him squirt more ketchup. His taste in food needed work.

Charlotte, followed by her minion Misty, entered the cafeteria. Heads turned to look at them. "I'll bet you three hundred dollars that they sit right there," Darbie said, pointing at the table right in the middle of the cafeteria.

"You don't have three hundred dollars," Hannah said. "You shouldn't make a bet you can't pay."

"I guess. But I still think they're going to sit there." Darbie forked a chunk of Salisbury steak, dipped it in her mashed potatoes, and sank it into her mouth. "Mmm." She sighed.

Hannah and I watched with a mixture of shock and nausea.

"What?" she said through her full mouth. "Kell, I think you're an amazing cook, you know that. But you should give this stuff a chance."

Hannah let out a soft, "Yuck."

I said, "Someday I'm going to come back to this school and totally change this cafeteria. I'm going to make a different fabulous menu every day. Each week will have a theme: Mexican, breakfast-for-lunch, vegetarian, summer BBQ, stews and soups. It will be delicious and much healthier than that stuff." I pointed to the mashed potato–covered Twinkie Darbie was putting in her mouth.

Hannah said, "Years from now you're going to be a famous chef in a big city like Los Angeles, London, or Rome. You'll have your own magazine and TV show, like Felice Foudini. Maybe she'll retire and you can take all her fans. You're not going to have time for the Alfred Nobel cafeteria."

I sighed, thinking of the wonderful dream Hannah had painted for my future. "Speaking of cooking, ask yourselves: What do you get when you mix an ancient book of secret recipes hidden in a 1953 encyclopedia, two mysterious warnings, unusual ingredients from a spooky store owned by a kook, and three BFFs?"

They didn't know.

I answered: "A *secret* cooking club."

"SECRET cooking club!" Darbie exclaimed with a spittle of Twinkie crumbs, just as Charlotte Barney was walking by with her lunch tray.

Charlotte stopped and said very loudly (on purpose), "SECRET COOKING CLUB! Hey, everyone! Kelly Quinn and her friends have a SECRET COOKING CLUB! Hahahaha!" She laughed all the way to the boys' table, Misty on her heels.

They wiggled themselves into seats next to Frankie and Tony, laughing the whole time. After setting their trays down, they high-tenned across the table.

Darbie sank into her chair. My fist tightened around my fork until my knuckles were white. "Sorry," she said. The remaining Twinkie found its way into her cheeks.

My face was consumed by a red blush, and my eyes were coated with a heavy glaze of fog. I blinked and cleared them just enough to see Frankie and Tony looking my way. They weren't laughing.

7

Shoobedoobedoowhop

Charlotte called to me as I raced ahead of her off the bus, "Where are you going in such a hurry, Kelly Quinn?"

I continued to hustle home, not answering.

Everyone wanted to be Charlotte's friend. She always had the best toys and clothes. What people didn't know was that the *idea* of hanging out with Charlotte was always better than *actually* hanging out with her.

It all started in third grade. Charlotte and I decided to jump rope. We tied one end around a tree and I turned and turned for her until my arm felt like it was going to drop off at the shoulder.

I wanted to jump, but she wouldn't give me my chance.

Then Darbie asked if she could play too. "No, Freckle Juice. Go away," Charlotte said. And Darbie cried. Charlotte said to her, "Go play with the kindergarteners, you baby."

That's when Hannah came over and also wanted to play.

Charlotte (who was jumping this whole time) laughed and said to Hannah, "You're too tall. We can't turn the rope high enough to get it over your head."

I said, "This would be better with more kids."

She said, "Shut up, Kelly Quinn. My mom says I have to be best friends with you because you live next door. But, she didn't say anything about those two losers."

That was the moment she became my rival.

She has been my rival ever since then—and has gotten worse (please refer back to ninth birthday party). I tried to convince myself that a relationship with her *builds character*. That's what my dad would say about doing things you don't like, and he knew what he was talking about because my mom always makes him do things that he didnt't like.

"I'm talking to you, Kelly Quinn." She always used my last name as though I might not know I was the Kelly she was beckoning. I quickly walked toward home so I could get ready for the club's first meeting.

"Are you heading to your *secret* club?"

My face got hot, and I clenched my hands. She was just evil. It took all my strength, but I ignored her.

Darbie and Hannah arrived on time. Hannah on foot, Darbie on Rollerblades.

"How did you do?" Mom asked.

Darbie looked at her watch before untying her Rollerblades. "Seven minutes, fifty-eight seconds," she said. It took Darbie about eight minutes to skate from her house to mine and she was always trying to make it faster.

We ditched Mom and secluded ourselves in my bedroom. Darbie flopped onto my flowered comforter and checked out the new posters on the walls. "Where did you get all these?" she asked.

"I joined the Felice Foudini fan club and sent in ten dollars. They sent me back a big envelope of pictures. I love this one," I said, pointing at the poster of a layered cake designed by Felice. Each layer was a different color hinting at its flavor. "I can only imagine what one perfect bite of that tastes like," I said. "See this light brown layer? I think that's cappuccino. I imagine the dark brown one is Swiss chocolate, the creamy colored layer is French vanilla, and this golden one is a really moist carrot cake. And the last layer is a thick whipped cream spread."

Darbie asked, "Did you just make that up?"

"Yeah. I was lying in bed staring at it, and that's what I imagined it was."

Hannah said, "I think I gained a pound just listening."

Darbie rolled her eyes. "Pounds, schmounds."

Bud came running into my room wearing Dad's work boots, a bicycle helmet, a Batman cape, and a snorkel in his mouth. He sang "The Wheels on the Bus" as loud as he could.

"MOM! TELL BUD TO GET OUT OF MY ROOM!"

"Maybe there's a recipe to make little brothers disappear," Darbie said under her breath.

"Now, *that* would be awesome," Hannah said.

Bud started jumping on my bed. "MooOOM!"

My mother came rushing in with a paper shopping bag over her arm. "Kelly Quinn, please don't yell like that unless someone is bleeding." She waved the bag at Bud and said, "You, scoot. Play downstairs."

Bud left, still singing at the top of his lungs.

"And don't come back!" I yelled after him. The little rat turned around and stuck out his tongue.

Mom hung around. I cleared my throat, signaling her to leave. "Oh," she said, getting the hint. She scurried outside my bedroom door, picked something up, and scurried back in. It was a shopping bag from The Kitchen Sink, a fancy cooking supply store at the mall. "I thought that members of a real cooking club, secret or not, should have matching aprons!" She took four aprons out of the bag. They were long and covered with tomatoes.

"Why do you have an extra one?" Hannah asked, sweeping her hair into a ponytail holder.

"I thought this one could be mine," Mom said.

"Mom, you said you'd leave us alone." I couldn't believe I had to remind her of this.

"Oh, I'm just kidding. I'll hang this on a hook in the pantry in case you ever invite someone else to join your club." The bag made a crunching sound when she put the apron in it. "Hey, I saw Charlotte walking home from the bus stop. Maybe she'd like to come over and join you girls."

The sideways glance I gave her reminded her of how I feel about Charlotte Barney.

"Oh, all right. Call me if you need help. And make sure you use the special oven mitts that go high up your arms, and don't lick the spoon if it's touched raw meat or egg, and be very, very careful if you chop anything. I don't want to send anyone home with nine fingers. And be careful—"

"Mom," I interrupted. "We get it."

"Okay, okay, okay." She pulled the door shut behind herself.

"I thought she'd never leave," I said.

Hannah was admiring her apron. "You have to admit, Kell, these are very Primetime Food TV."

Darbie asked, "You aren't seriously thinking of inviting Charlotte, are you?"

"No way!" I said. "Let's get the first meeting of our *secret* cooking club called to order. This means we can't tell anybody."

"Why does it have to be a secret?" Hannah asked. "I mean, we're in seventh grade now. Isn't that a little silly?"

I was really surprised and a little hurt to hear Hannah say that.

Hannah continued, "It's not like we're doing anything illegal. Are we?"

"Well," I said. "One reason is that it's a good thing if Charlotte doesn't know."

"Weren't you in the cafeteria today?" Hannah balked. "*Everyone* knows!"

"But they don't need to know any *more*. Especially Charlotte! She'll ruin everything. Do I need to remind you of the surprise party catastrophe?" I spared them from hearing me whine about the event again.

"*And* . . ." I reached under my bed and whipped out the Secret Recipe Book. "The club is secret because we're going to use recipes from this book."

"But that book is cursed. Remember?" Darbie asked.

"You think that's possible?" I replied.

Hannah dotted gloss on her lips. "No. It's not possible."

Darbie said, "But the warnings. What were they?"

I reminded her. "'Beware of the Law of Returns,' and

the thing Señora Perez said—'You get what you deserve.'"

Darbie said, "Well, something beginning with 'Beware' usually indicates that you're supposed to watch out, like 'Beware of Attack Dog.' If you go on that property, the dog will eat you."

"I think you're taking it a little too seriously," Hannah said. "The paper in the Book could've been anything. I'm always sticking all kinds of papers in my books. And Señora Perez is a strange old lady. I wouldn't worry about something she said."

"What do you think?" I asked Darbie.

"Well, I guess it's okay. And if not, we'll have an exciting story to tell—if we're still alive. But if we don't start cooking soon, you'll have to beware of me," Darbie said. "because I'm starvin' like Marvin, *amigas*."

"First," I said, "I was thinking we need a secret handshake. Maybe something like this." I showed them a grip I'd made up. It ended with high fives. The girls tried it, although Hannah blew her bangs out of her face the whole time, signaling to me that she was bored or annoyed. In this instance, maybe she was both.

"I like that," Darbie said. She and Hannah did it again.

Hannah said, "Okay, I've got it. So now can we decide what we're going to make, or do we need a password, too?"

"Great idea," I said.

"I was only kidding." Hannah blew her bangs again.

Darbie asked, "How about 'shoobedoobedoowhop'?"

Hannah didn't seem to care.

"Fine. Shoobedoobedoowhop it is," I said.

"So." I flipped through the Book. "I've checked out this book, and something you guys said earlier gave me an idea." I turned to a page and pointed to Keeps 'Em Quiet Cobbler. There was a note at the bottom of the page: Stopped the *gallo* from his early morning cockle, *ip.*

"What's *gallo*?" Darbie asked.

Hannah answered, "That's Spanish for 'rooster.'"

I asked, "What's *ip*?'

"I don't know. But I don't think it matters," Hannah said. "You can still tell what the note means: Stopped the rooster from its cockle. It's nonsense, Kell."

I said, "Maybe not. We were talking about someone who is loud and annoying"—Darbie's eyebrows lifted like she knew what I was about to say—"and how we would want to shut him up. You know what I'm thinking?"

Darbie asked, "You think if we make this cobbler and feed it to Bud that he'll shut up?"

I shrugged my shoulders in an "I dunno but it's worth a try" kind of way.

"I'm game," Darbie said.

I pointed on the page to a strange ingredient, aged

vetivert stems. "I have them in here." I found it in the bag of items I'd bought from La Cocina.

We looked closely at the bottle. The glass was so thick, it distorted the contents. They looked wavy, like they were under water. I pulled hard at the cork in the top. It made a distinctive popping sound when it was freed from the bottle. I took out a few stems. I smelled them, but they were odorless.

"What do you think it is?" Kelly asked.

"Looks like plant stems," Hannah offered.

"Maybe we should look it up before we try to feed it to my little brother. He's a pain in the rumpus, but we don't want to kill him."

Darbie, the Queen of Google, clicked on my desktop until she found "vetivert." "It says here that it's a tall grass whose roots and leaves are often used in alternative healing. What's alternative healing?"

I said, "That's like when you don't go to the doctor or use regular medicine. Instead you take vitamins and use natural stuff to help you feel better or to prevent getting sick."

Hannah looked at me, puzzled. "How do you know that?"

"My aunt is into some of that stuff," I explained. "She's a vegetarian, she does yoga every day, and she doesn't shave her legs. When we go to her house she makes my family meditate. My dad falls asleep. Worst of all, she doesn't have a TV. Could you imagine life without *The Pastry Quartet*, *Don't Let This Happen to Your Kitchen*, or *Fab Food with Felice Foudini*?"

"And now back to reality," Hannah said. "From that description, it doesn't look like this spice will kill your brother. But if it does, and we're accused of murder, I was never here. Got it?"

"Got it," I said.

"Got it," said Darbie. "Kell, if we go to juvie, will you be my roommate?"

"You know it!"

"Cool."

"All right," I said. "Cobbler it is. We just got some apples from Mrs. Silvers. I had one for lunch and it was really awesome."

"You got them from Mrs. Silvers, the witch?" Darbie asked.

"Yes. But seriously, they're delish. So I guess we're all set," I said, heading out the door. "Come on Shoobedoobedoowhops. Let's go cook."

8

Cobbler

Question: *What do you get when you combine an annoying little brother with a secret cooking club?*

Answer: *A taste-tester.*

Outfitted in our new aprons, we spread out the kitchen tools and started peeling apples.

BANG! CRASH! CLANG! Pots and pans clanged outside the kitchen. Bud was marching around, in and out of the kitchen, banging on pots like drums. He yelled as loud as he could, "Kelly is smelly and so are her friends!"

CLANG! CLINK! CRASH!

Darbie picked up a banana, peeled it, and took a bite. "Kelly Quinn, I might stick this up his nose if he doesn't zip his pie hole."

CRASH! "Kelly is smelly! And her friends stink too!"

"Let's get to work and see if this cobbler really does keep 'em quiet," I said. Then I yelled, "MOOOOooom!"

My mom called into the kitchen. "Mister, you're going to Time Out!" We heard Bud drag the pans across the hard wood floor to the Time-Out chair.

Hannah took her hands off her ears. "Thank goodness."

I pushed preheat on the oven and cracked open the *World Book Encyclopedia, Volume T.* Carefully, I turned each worn page until I got to the cobbler. I dragged my finger over the handwritten recipe. "I wonder who wrote this," I said.

Neither of the girls answered, giving me a minute to wonder about the recipe book's writer. The windows steamed up from the heat growing in the kitchen. I cracked one open. I felt a cool breeze and noticed dark clouds rolling in. Suddenly I felt like Darbie, Hannah, and I weren't the only ones in my kitchen—I had the bizarre feeling that whoever wrote the Book was there with us. The thought gave me a chill.

"What do we need, Kell?" Darbie asked.

Hannah's pink-nail-polished index finger brushed along the ingredient list. She called out the items while Darbie pulled them out of the pantry and set them on the countertop. Hannah concluded with, "And aged vetivert stems."

I took the little bottle from my apron pocket and set it on the countertop.

The girls sliced apples, measured, and stirred. I fluffed together the flour, sugar, and softened butter with a fork.

Darbie added the vetivert. I thought maybe the mixture would bubble over or explode or turn a psychedelic color, but it looked like ordinary apple goop. Actually, it looked like rich, delectable apple goop. It was cinnamonny brown and looked delicious next to the creamy flour-sugar-butter mixture. I imagined what it was going to look like hot and bubbly from the oven.

Darbie poured the apple goop into a pan.

Hannah sprinkled the flour-sugar-butter mixture I'd made atop the goop. "This looks awesome," she said.

I slid the pan into the oven, wearing huge heat-resistant gloves. Soon the kitchen filled with wonderful apple smells. At the same time, the skyline became covered with gray clouds. We turned on the oven's interior light and watched the cobbler bake, like we were watching TV.

"I'm freaking out a little about soccer tryouts this year," Darbie said, staring at the oven.

"You'll be fine," Hannah said.

"That's easy for you to say. You're in great shape from swimming all summer and you were one of the best players on the team last year," Darbie said. "If you haven't noticed," she added, "I'm not the most coordinated person in the world."

"Just try your best and work really hard. Coach Richards likes that," Hannah said.

My mind was in the hot oven, in the sizzling pan, in the sugary mixture gurgling over the rim, and in the drops that dropped onto the bottom of the oven. "Who do you think wrote it?" I asked.

"What?" Hannah asked.

"The Book."

The girls didn't have an answer. I was deep in thought about it when there was a knock at the back door. I looked out and saw a blond head. If I looked a little closer, I might have found little red horns under the curly locks.

"Argh," Darbie groaned when she saw Charlotte. When we didn't move toward the door, Hannah opened it. Charlotte pushed past her and into the kitchen. I subtly took a dishcloth and tossed it over the encyclopedia.

"What do you want?" I asked.

Charlotte scanned the kitchen. Her nose lifted slightly. "Wait a minute. Is this is your silly little secret club?" she asked with a laugh and a snort.

"WHAT do you want?" I asked again impatiently.

"I brought this letter. It came to our house. It's for your mom, from a reunion company in Massachusetts. Probably her high school reunion."

"Thanks for bringing it," I said as I escorted her to the back door. "I'll make sure my mom gets it." I practically shoved her onto the driveway.

"You're so rude, Kelly Quinn."

Darbie said, real sarcastically, "Thanks for coming. Been great seeing you. Have a super night. Always a pleasure."

Charlotte snapped, "This club is so stupid, and I don't know what you're making, but it smells terrible because you're a terrible cook, Kelly Quinn. And I hope you and your mom lose the chili contest *again* this year."

I slammed the door.

"Grrr. She is so MEAN," I said.

"Just ignore her," Hannah said. "She's probably jealous that we didn't invite her."

I said, "Why would she want—" *Beep! Beep! Beep!* The oven timer went off.

"Woot! Woot! Shoobedoobedoowhop!" Darbie called. "My ribs are showing, let me at that bad boy."

I slid the pan out of the oven and set it on a trivet. We all leaned over the dessert and inhaled. It smelled *delicioso!*

A pile of leaves rustled in a strange way, drawing our attention outside, where Charlotte was standing in the light rain, watching us. When she saw that we'd caught her little spy thing, she headed home.

"She's unbelievable," I said.

Darbie pulled the blinds down. "What's the hold-up?" she asked. "Fork, please."

"Well," I said. "I'm dying to taste it too. But, if it's meant to 'keep 'em quiet,' I don't know if we should. I mean, what would happen to us?"

Darbie said, "You could've mentioned that earlier, before I became so weak with hunger that I can hardly rip open a package of Twinkies."

Suddenly, a crack of thunder shook the house. *BOOM!*

I asked, "What was that?"

"Just thunder," Hannah said.

Darbie said, "It's the warning. I told you that book was cursed. We were warned!"

KABOOM!

We shrieked and Mom came in. "Everything okay?" she asked, shutting the oven door.

"Yeah. The thunder scared us," I said.

"Me too." She inspected the dish. "Oh, girls, this looks so good."

Headlights glided into our driveway. "That looks like my mom's car," Darbie said. Even though she lives just a block away, Darbie isn't allowed to skate home in the dark or the rain. "I'm outta here. Barb is making stuffed meat-loaf tonight." (Darbie was the only kid I knew who called her mom by her first name.)

"Why don't you grab your books. I'll get some containers

and you can all take some of this scrumptious-looking cobbler home," Mom offered.

"Ummm." Darbie looked at Hannah and me. "No. No thanks, Mrs. Q. I'm stuffed."

"No?" Mom asked, confused.

"No," Darbie said. "We were thinking . . . thinking, umm—"

"Thinking that you would have it with dinner tonight," Hannah helped.

"That's a wonderful idea," Mom said. "Thanks, girls."

We saw another set of headlights pull into the driveway. "That looks like my dad's car." Hannah said. She joined Darbie in getting her things and the two dashed into the rain.

It was just Mom and me. She said, "Mrs. Silvers called. She wanted to know if you—"

"I know, I know. I'm going." I went across the street with an umbrella and a pooper-scooper.

That night's Quinn Family Dinner was typical, except for the addition of a dish made from a Secret Recipe Book for the purpose of shutting up my little brother.

Rosey ate dry food out of her bowl on the floor next to the table while Mom served dessert. She dished out the cobbler, starting with my brother, who sniffed in a huge breath and let out a huge, spitty sneeze all over the rest of the pan.

Presto! Cobbler a la snot.

"Bud! Cover your mouth!" Mom scolded. He wiped his nose on his sleeve.

I passed on eating the germ-infested cobbler. Mom too. Dad scooped a mountain onto his plate.

"Ah, Dad. You sure you want that? I mean, you might get sick," I said.

"Nonsense," he said. "Dads don't get sick." He shoveled a big bite of cobbler into his mouth.

"Mmmmmm. You and your friends made this?" Dad asked.

"Yup," I said.

"With the apples from Mrs. Silvers," Mom added.

Dad stopped with his fork in midair. "Did you check them for poison?

9

Roller Darbie

Coach Richards is both the soccer coach and my science teacher. He's young, not much older than Vinny Rusamano, Frankie and Tony's older brother, who's in his second year of college.

He sat us alphabetically, which put Charlotte right in front and Hannah a few seats behind her. The second row included Darbie, me, Frankie, and Tony Rusamano. Obviously, the second row is the best one—if only "Hernandez" was later in the alphabet.

We stared at Coach, who explained the scientific process while sipping his carrot juice. "You'll come up with a hypothesis. And then we'll work in the lab and conduct experiments to either prove or disprove your theory. Any questions?"

None.

"Now turn to page thirty-three," he said. "We're going to talk about Newton's Third Law. Does anyone know what that is?"

No one reacted.

"Newton says . . ." Coach Richards wrote on the board. The room was quiet except for the sound of scratching chalk.

Darbie leaned over. "The only Newton I'm interested in is Fig."

I got a little giggly.

Coach Richards read what he'd written. "For every action, there is an equal and opposite reaction." Maybe he could tell that we weren't impressed by Newton. He said, "Darbie, why don't you read out loud to us, starting at the top of the page."

Darbie read, but I don't think anyone paid attention, except for Hannah, who diligently took notes.

At the end of class Coach Richards invited any interested girls to come to soccer tryouts after school, which was when he transformed from science teacher into fitness maniac.

* * *

Coach Richards jogged around the back of the school to the soccer field wearing shorts and sneakers. We were already there waiting for him. "Have a seat and listen up!" he shouted, tucking his clipboard under his arm. We all think Coach Richards is a ten on the cutie scale, which only added to my stomach butterflies.

"I want to review a few rules for the newbies before we get tryouts started. Number one, you owe me a push-up for every minute you're late for practice." He gave Darbie a look. "Number two, you cannot practice or play in any games if you don't maintain a B average. Number three, if you're injured, you will come to practice and games suited up and you will stretch with and cheer for your teammates."

"There are more rules, but that's enough for now." He tossed his clipboard onto the grass and bent down to touch his toes. We did the same. "We'll do a lot of conditioning today. If you spent the summer eating Super Swirleys, this won't be easy. But we WILL have fun! . . . just probably not today." He grabbed the backs of his calves and pulled himself lower. The muscles in his forearms bulged like he had spent the whole summer lifting very heavy things. The man probably hadn't had a Swirley in his whole life. He looked more like the whole wheat type.

"Alrighty then. Let's start with a six-lap warm-up. The last five girls to finish will do an extra lap." He led the run. "LET'S MOVE IT, LADIES!"

We all ran after Coach Richards like chicks following their mother hen—a strong, science-y mother hen. He turned and ran backward so he could talk to us. "After the warm-up, we'll sprint, weave the bleachers, practice throw-ins, and we'll end with sit-ups."

I was already out of breath. I looked back and saw that Darbie was the caboose. Everyone was vying for the space right behind Coach, but Hannah had it, followed by Charlotte.

Question: *How many laps can Coach make Kelly Quinn run before she barfs?*

I guessed I would answer myself later, but I felt confident that Darbie would toss her cafeteria fried chicken, creamed corn, and Devil Dog before my lunch came up.

"PUSH IT!" Coach Richards yelled. He picked up a plastic orange cone from the sideline and yelled through it. "Push it, girls! No pain, no gain. Come on, Darbie O'Brien!"

Hannah fell back to talk to me. "How're you doing, Kell?" Even Hannah's soccer clothes were fashionable: rolled below the waist nylon shorts and a shirt bearing the Nike Swoosh.

"I'm dying, Shoobedoo. You know CPR?" I could hardly get the words out.

Charlotte had finished the first several laps hardly breaking a sweat. "Looking good, Kell," she said with her classic sarcastic snort. Hannah caught up to her and the two of them ran together for the rest of the tryout, which seemed to go on forever. Shockingly, it was only four o'clock when we were done.

Darbie's mom drove us all home after practice and we planned to reassemble at my house for a cooking club meeting at five.

Take:
1 sore throat
1 honey drop
A bag of frozen peas
A wicked radar system

Directions:
Knead. Let rise until ready.

I dropped my school stuff and sniffed the air. Something yucky lingered. "Mom, what's that smell?"

"I was trying some new combos with my chili." She whispered, "Let's just say, it didn't go well."

"I guess not," I said.

"Shhh," Mom said. "Buddy came home from school sick with a sore throat. He can hardly talk. He's resting, so you have to be very quiet."

"He can't talk?" I asked loudly.

"Shhh! That's right. You need to be quiet," Mom said.

I whispered, "He can't talk?"

"That's what I said. When are the girls coming over?"

I looked at my watch, "Any minute."

Darbie pushed my front door open. She tripped on her Rollerblades and fell on the tile floor.

"Skates off in the house," my mom whispered, then looked at Darbie more closely. She had blood on her face and her sweatshirt. "Oh my goodness." My mom rushed over and grabbed Darbie's face in her hands. "Come over to the sink."

My mom washed Darbie's face. "What happened, honey?"

"I was trying to skate fast, but my legs are so tired, I wiped out like a cowboy surfing the coral reef."

"Man, you're gonna have a big fat lip," I said.

"Kelly, please grab a bag of vegetables out of the freezer to put on her eye." Mom wiped the scratches on Darbie's legs. I could tell which areas would soon become black and blue.

"It'll make you look real tough for soccer," I said, but this didn't seem to make Darbie feel better. I handed her a bag of peas and searched my brain for something that might cheer her up. "Bud came home from school early today with a sore throat. He can hardly talk."

Darbie took the frozen peas off her face and looked at me with a twinkle in her swollen eye. "He lost his voice?"

I nodded.

"You're kidding!"

"Nope." When my mom wasn't looking, she gave me a thumbs-up.

"Darbie, maybe I should take you home," Mom said.

"Oh, can I stay, please? Really, I'm hunky-dory. We have something *very* important to cook."

"Well, if you have something *very* important to cook, that changes everything." Mom teased Darbie. "I'll call your mom and see what she says."

There was a beep in Mom's pocket. She pulled out her cell phone and flipped it open to read a text. "Oh, great. Your dad has no voice either. He's on his way home." She opened the fridge and took out the two containers of left-over apple cobbler. "I'm sorry, girls. I saved this cobbler for you from the unsneezed-on side of the pan, but I don't think you should eat it." Mom dumped the contents into the garbage disposal and flipped the switch. "I'm going to check on Bud. And don't worry, I'll keep the germs upstairs." She opened a small cabinet over the oven, got up on her tippy toes, and reached in for a tiny golden tin bearing a bumble-bee logo.

"What's that?" I asked, studying the label. The bee was interesting because it was wearing a sombrero.

"It's Moon Honey. I always keep a tin around for just such a situation. My mother swore these little drops would heal anything." She shook the tin. There was a slight rattle. She looked inside. "Only two left." She disappeared and

Hannah came in through the back door wearing plaid lounge pants and a Gap hoodie I'd never seen before.

When did she get all these new clothes?

Her hair was clean and damp, twisted up in a clip. Darbie and I were still sweaty and in our soccer clothes.

"Eew, what happened?" she asked when she saw Darbie.

Darbie, her head tilted back and her face covered with the bag of peas, quickly filled Hannah in on her fall, but she was more excited to tell her about my dad and Bud.

"Bud ate the cobbler?" Hannah asked.

"Yep," I confirmed.

"Wow," Hannah said. "That's so weird. That's what the note by the recipe said."

"You took the words right out of my mouth," Darbie said. "Which is empty, by the way. And this is a problem because I just got a text message from my stomach saying 'put food here, *por favor.*'" She pointed to her stomach.

I unwrapped a stick of string cheese and shoved it under the peas and into Darbie's mouth. She took a generous bite and held it like a microphone. "Thank you, Shoobedoobedoowhop," she said into the string cheese.

Hannah squinted like she was concentrating. "And your dad lost his voice too. Why didn't you?"

I explained the sneeze infestation.

"This is way whacked out, doncha think?" Darbie asked,

her mouth full of string cheese. "It happened just like it did for the rooster."

Hannah said, "I have to admit, it's a little coincidental."

"My mom watches a lot of crime shows on TV and the investigators always say there is no such thing as coincidence," I said.

"This might be a good time for me to point out that we're not on a TV crime show," Hannah said. "There could be a million reasons why Bud and Mr. Quinn are sick. Maybe they have a cold. Colds are very common. That's why they're called 'common colds.' People get them all the time."

"That's not a million reasons," Darbie said. "That's one."

"You get the point." Hannah blew her blond bangs out of her face. She was frustrated with Darbie already.

I tried to change the subject so we didn't start fighting. "Ready?"

"For what?" Hannah asked.

"We're a cooking club, aren't we?" I pulled my apron over my head. "I've been doing some thinking and—"

There was a knock on the back door. I saw a curly mane in the door's window. "You've got to be kidding me. She must have some kind of wicked radar system." I went to the door, but this time I was careful to stand in front of it so Charlotte couldn't just walk in. "May I help you?"

"Actually, you can. Do you have any clear nail polish?"

"Nail polish?"

"Yeah, I ran out in the middle of doing my nails." She tried to be nonchalant when she stretched her head to the right and left, but I could tell she was trying to see what we were doing in the kitchen.

I looked at her hands. "They don't look wet."

"Um, my toenails."

I looked down. She wore sandals, and there was some polish on her toes that I suspected was also dry.

"No. I don't have any clear polish."

"What's that smell?" Charlotte asked. "Is that chili?" I didn't answer. "Gross. Maybe you shouldn't even bother to enter this year. Honestly, I don't understand why anyone would go to all the trouble of making something you could buy already made. Seems like a waste of time. And it seems stupid to enter a contest you know you're going to *lose*."

I had successfully blocked Charlotte so she couldn't see Darbie. But she heard Darbie when she yelled, "Wanna make a bet?"

Charlotte asked me, even though I wasn't the one who asked the question, "*You* want to make *me* a bet that *you'll* win the chili contest?"

"Yep," Darbie yelled.

"Oh, you're so on. What did you have in mind?" she asked me.

I opened my mouth to answer, but Darbie beat me to it. From her kitchen chair she yelled, "If Kelly wins, you have to rake her yard. If Kelly loses, she'll rake your yard."

Charlotte grabbed my hand and shook it. "It's a bet, Kelly Quinn." She followed the beaten path back to her house.

I slammed the door and walked over to Darbie, whose eyes were buried under a bag of frozen peas. I propped my hands on my hips. "What did you do that for?"

The peas fell into her lap when she lifted her head. "What?"

"That bet. Are you crazy?" I asked.

Hannah chimed in, "Mrs. Rusamano is on a four-year winning streak. You and your mom are good cooks, but Mrs. R. is great." Hannah was right, but it would have been nice if she was a little more optimistic about our chances of winning.

Darbie picked up the encyclopedia with her bandaged hand. "Have you forgotten that you have an ancient secret recipedia?"

The corners of my lips started to bend, and suddenly I wasn't so mad at Darbie.

10

Hexberry Tarta

"If the Book can make Bud lose his voice, then it should be able to help you win a chili contest," Darbie said.

I smiled because I liked what Darbie was saying, but it also gave me another idea. "And, maybe it can take care of a nasty, curly-haired, soccer-playing, chili-contest-betting, clear-nail-polish-needing, head-in-the-back-door-snooping girl?"

Darbie looked right at me. She pointed to me and then to her and to me again. "You and me," she said. "We think so much alike, it scares me. And I don't scare easily. Except for vampires, and werewolves, and zombies, and tsunamis, and earthquakes, and—"

"We get it," Hannah said. "Lucky for you there's no such thing as monsters and we live in Delaware, so we don't have those kinds of natural disasters."

"But I was also going to mention that I'm not too crazy about cryptic warnings," Darbie said. "Remember 'You get what you deserve'? Do we deserve something for potioning Bud?"

"You're taking this warning stuff too seriously, Darb," Hannah said.

"Lucky for me I have you, Hannah Happygolucky, to bring me back to reality." Darbie tilted her head back again and dropped the bag of peas on her face. "If you're not worried, then I'm not either."

Hannah picked up the Book. I saw her fingertips rub the encyclopedia's rough cover. "So, what can we cook up for Charlotte?"

"I thought you thought it was all coincidence," I said.

"Oh, I do," Hannah said. "But, I also support the process of scientific experimentation. And I think Charlotte was really mean to you just now with all that 'you shouldn't even enter the contest' stuff. I think she'd make a good test subject. Whatcha got in that recipedia?"

"Secret Recipe Book," I corrected her. We looked through the pages together. I was glad Hannah Happygolucky wasn't blowing her bangs out of her face or rolling her eyes. It felt like the three of us were in this together.

Hannah read aloud, "Lavender *Bizcocho de Chocolate*. That's Lavender Chocolate Brownie: Whoever eats this becomes *muy relajado*—*ip*. That's very relaxed."

"What's *ip*?" I asked.

"I still don't know that word. I'm not sure it even is a word," Hannah said. "Condensed Chamomile *Té*: If you need to fall asleep *muy rápido*. That's 'quickly.'" She turned a page. "Hexberry *Tarta. Embrujar*—*ip*. There's *ip* again. I'm gonna have to look that up, it's bothering me that I don't know it means."

I asked, "What's *tarta* and *embrujar*?"

"*Tarta* is 'pie,'" Hannah said. "*Embrujar* is the verb 'to hex.'"

Darbie said, "B-I-N-G-O, and Charlotte was her name-o. That's what she needs, an H-E-X."

"What are the ingredients? I'll check to see if we have everything," I said.

I rifled through the freezer and found some pre-made pie crust. I held the bag up. "I can name that tune in two notes: *pre-made*."

"Let's see." Hannah read. "Sugar?"

"Check."

"Lemon juice, flour, cinnamon, unsalted butter?"

"Check, check, check, check."

"Shaved hazelnuts?"

"Check."

"Really?" Hannah asked, "You keep shaved hazelnuts in the house?"

"I never met a hazelnut I didn't like," Darbie said, the bag of peas now defrosting and dripping cold water down her cheeks. She wiped the drops with her shirt.

"We have hazelnuts. I like to roast them with oil, garlic, and cayenne pepper and mix them with vegetables," I said.

"Okay then," Hannah said. "Rue seed?"

Darbie asked, "What seed?"

"Rue seed," Hannah repeated. "That's what it says."

I went to my backpack and took out the brown paper bag from La Cocina. I looked at the yellow, green, and brown bottles and the plastic bag until I found the one with the rue. The seeds were very tiny, perfectly round and black. "Check."

"Great. The last thing is berries. It doesn't say what kind."

I stuck my head into the fridge. I thought I saw blue-berries in here yesterday," I said. I kept searching. "Mom!" I yelled loud enough for her to hear me upstairs . . . or in Canada.

"I'm right here." She answered me from the other side of the kitchen where she was standing with the phone stuck in the crook of her neck. "And don't yell." I looked at Hannah with bulgy eyes and a tilted head. She got the hint because she tucked the recipe book under her butt. Mom looked at Darbie. "Darbie, your mom says you can stay, but she's picking you up at six o'clock."

"Mom, where are the blueberries?"

"Dad ate them," she said, then continued talking to Darbie's mom.

"Great. No berries," I said.

Mom interrupted, "And Darbie, your mom wants to know if you broke your record."

Darbie shook her head. "Nah, not even close. My legs are like Jell-O from soccer."

"Maybe we can substitute something else," I said, thinking out loud. "Felice does that all the time."

"Darbie, your mom also mentioned I can call you 'Roller Darbie,'" my mom said. "You know, like roller derby?" We didn't laugh. "You girls have no sense of humor," she said. She said good-bye to Darbie's mom and looked at all the stuff on the table. Her eyes stopped on the small amber bottle of rue seed. "What's that?"

The antique bottle stuck out like Darbie at a science fair. "It's a spice for this pie we're going to make. I got it at La Cocina."

She nodded. "Why don't you use blackberries?"

I looked out the back window toward the Barneys' backyard. "That would mean we'd have to go into her lair."

"Don't be dramatic," Mom said. "Besides, I saw her leave

a few minutes ago. Her dad mentioned to me this morning that she was going to get new cleats."

"Then, blackberries it is," I said. "You ready to pick?"

Darbie said, "You two go. I'll just sit here with frozen peas on my face and wait for you."

As expected, Mrs. Barney let us pick all the berries we wanted. We picked as fast as we could, hoping to return to the safety of my house before the devil girl got home.

I was no fortune-teller, but I could have predicted what would happen next. Charlotte Barney came around the back of her house wearing brand-spanking-new cleats.

Hands on her hips she said, "What are you doing in my backyard?"

Just then my back door opened and Darbie appeared. "You guys almost done? My face is getting frostbite."

Charlotte gasped and put her hand over her mouth. Darbie's lips were puffy, her eye was black and blue, and there was a scratch on her cheek. "What the heck ran over you?"

I thought up a lie before Darbie could speak. "It was Mrs. Silvers. She put a spell on Darbie for Rollerblading past her house!" I inched closer to my back door, nudging Hannah with me. "That witch came outside and waved her arms all around. Bats came out of the trees, attacked Darbie, and left her like this."

Charlotte folded her arms across her chest and said, "Kelly Quinn, you are a big liar. You're a bad soccer player, a terrible cook, and a horrible liar. Just so you know, I'm not going to talk to any of you at soccer tomorrow."

"*No problemo*," Darbie said, and slammed the door once Hannah and I were safely inside with the berries.

"I swear she knew exactly what time to come home. It's like some kind of mean girl sixth sense," I said.

I put the berries into the sink and rinsed them. Then we mixed the pie filling, adding the clean berries.

"Did you notice her new cleats?" Hannah asked, as if we could have missed the shine of the hot pink laces.

We mixed and stirred and blended. "Ya-hoo for the new cleats." Darbie twirled her finger in the air.

Hannah asked, "Have you seen her outside practicing?" Hannah was the best player on our soccer team, the Alfred Noble School ANtS, but Charlotte was second-best.

"No—and don't look now, but there she goes. Probably breaking in her new cleats." I nodded toward the window that looked out to the front of the house. We saw Charlotte run down the street, her bouncy ponytail jumping up and down on top of her head. Her pink laces sparkled.

"That can take a while," Hannah added. "I know a girl who brought new cleats to soccer camp and got terrible blisters. You need to do it gradually and wear extra socks for a few weeks."

"It would be a shame if those fancy-schmancy cleats hurt Charlotte's feet," Darbie said.

I chuckled. "Yeah right."

"Or worse, it looks like the groovy new cleats might get caught in the rain. Uh-oh, they might not be shiny anymore," Darbie said, looking at the dark clouds rolling in.

The pie filling became smooth. I picked up the amber bottle. The cork made a *pop* when I pulled it out. "How much rue seed does it say to add?" I asked Hannah.

"It says a dash," she answered. "That's not very precise,"

I pinched some seeds between my thumb and middle finger. Then over the bowl of filling I rolled my fingers together, letting go of a few seeds at a time. They looked like teeny pebbles plopping into blackberry-colored quicksand. When Hannah stirred, they sunk in and disappeared.

"It's ready," I said.

Hannah looked out the front window and saw the pink laces sprinting up the street as if on cue. "Here she comes." Charlotte got to her front stoop. "Home safe and sound."

Rain drops splashed against the kitchen windows.

While the oven preheated, we loaded the dirty dishes into the washer.

Suddenly, a bright light filled the room and a bolt of lightning struck so close we all gasped.

From outside we heard a *creak*, a *crack*, and a *CRASH!* and we saw my family's big old oak tree fall down, crashing right into the Barneys' backyard. At that same moment, the lights went out.

"Well," I said into the dim kitchen. "It doesn't look like we can bake this puppy—our oven is electric."

After the girls left, I washed up and tucked myself into bed. I wrote in my journal using only the light of the moon and a flashlight. Rosey was under the covers between my feet. My head rested on BunnyBun, my favorite stuffed toy. It felt like a rag was twisting in my gut. I knew why, but I couldn't believe it. It might be that I felt just a tiny bit badly about Bud's voice.

I closed my journal, took my flashlight and BunnyBun, and carefully found my way to Bud's room. I slid the beam of light onto his bed. He was sleeping. I set BunnyBun under the sheets next to him.

11

Blisters

Gather:

1 hex

1 fitness-crazed soccer coach

1 pair of brand-new cleats

11 sit-ups

1 black eye

Directions:

Shove into a squeezy water bottle and shake together until it explodes into Death By Humiliation.

D arn alarm clock!

Thanks to the electricity going out, I rushed around like a girl packing for a trip to Crazytown. I really didn't want to miss the bus on the third day of school.

"Kelly, wait," Mom said.

I sniffed. "What's that smell?"

"I hope you don't mind, but I baked the pie you girls made last night. I was thinking you could run it over to the Barneys' because I feel bad about the tree falling into their yard last night."

Hmm. Actually, that's perfect because I have to get the pie to Charlotte anyway.

"Sure. I'll take it over right now."

I scooped up the pie pan with a kitchen towel and took the path next door. Then a thought hit me.

I don't want to hex all the Barneys, just Charlotte. How am I going to do that?

Think, think, think.

What would Darbie do?

I got it!

I peeked in the back window and saw Mrs. Barney moving around the kitchen. She was dressed like one of those ladies on *Desperate Housewives.* I got my facial expression ready and made a distressing noise right outside their back door.

Mrs. Barney opened it. "What on Earth?" She saw me and three quarters of my fabulous Hexberry Pie on the ground. "Kelly Quinn, what happened? Are you all right?"

"Oh, I'm fine, Mrs. Barney," I said with just a hint of on-demand tears in my eyes. "But, my mom is going to kill me. She sent this delicious pie over for you because she feels so badly about the tree falling down."

"Well," Mrs. Barney said, "that tree should have been cut down a long time ago. It was just a matter of time."

"Yes, ma'am," I said with my saddest voice. "And stupid me, I dropped the pie. There's only one piece left. And I really wanted Charlotte to try it. I'm so sorry, please don't tell my mom."

"Oh, nonsense. I won't say anything." She took the dish from me. "Give me that. I'm packing Charlotte's lunch right now. I'll put the pie in it."

I wiped my pretend tears with the back of my hand. "Thanks Mrs. Barney, you're the best."

And off to the bus stop I went.

Operation Hexberry Pie? *Success.*

Charlotte got on the bus ahead of me, and over her shoulder she said, "Oh, thanks for the pie you made us with the blackberries that you stole from my yard."

"You're welcome," I said. "I hope you like it."

She sat in the very front seat. I headed to the back row. "If you ask me, that tree should've been taken down a long time ago," Charlotte called after me.

"You're probably right." I tilted my head and gave Charlotte a heartfelt smile.

"Oh, and my mom wants to know if you can feed the cat next weekend," Charlotte said. I feed their cat every weekend when they go to their beach house. Come to think of it, I'm kind of like the pet caretaker of Coyote Street.

"I'd love to. Enjoy the pie."

"LINE UP, LADIES! Let's stretch for today's run." Coach Richards's back was to us. He grabbed his foot behind his butt and bent down. I hopped closer to him to read the back of his shirt. It said UNIVERSITY OF DELAWARE ATHLETIC DEPARTMENT.

"And stretch your arms," he said, dropping his foot and turning around to find me in his personal space bubble. "Quinn?"

"Sorry, Coach. Um, I was, um, stretching really far and, umm . . ."

"Just get back over there."

"Okay." I moved back with the rest of the ANtS and I saw Darbie running down the hill, her shoes laces untied. She tripped and fell, got up, and ran down the rest of the way. Right behind her was Charlotte Barney, still in her school clothes, limping.

"You're late," Coach said to Darbie. He looked at his watch. "Rule number one: a push-up for each minute. Down on the ground and give me eleven." To Charlotte he said, "What's the *problemo* Barney? Why aren't you dressed for practice?"

She bent over and touched her feet. "Terrible blisters,

Coach. They're killing me like you couldn't believe."

Blisters?

"What's rule number three, girls?"

Go hex, go hex! Woot! Woot!

The girls chanted, "If you're injured, you come to the practice and games suited up and you will stretch with and cheer for your teammates."

"Excellent," Coach said. "Put your stuff on the bench and give me sit-ups till I tell you to stop. That won't hurt your blisters."

I sucked my bottom lip under my teeth, made fists, and did a little dance. In my head I was singing: *Go hex! She's doing lots of sit-ups! Woot! Woot!*

Coach said, "Quinn, what are you doing?"

I stopped my little dance. "Nothing, Coach, just excited to run, that's all."

"Good attitude. I like a good attitude, Quinn." Then he looked at Darbie, who was struggling with her push-ups. "Niiiiiine." She lowered her chin back down to the ground. "Tennnnnn." She lowered her chin again. "Elevvvennnnn." She flopped back down onto her belly before rolling onto her back.

Coach walked closer to Darbie. "Do me a favor and be late again next time, so we can work on those." He took off his sunglasses, tucked them into the neck of his

T-shirt, and examined Darbie's face. "I like the bruised look. Makes you look tough." Hands on hips, he assessed the troops and tucked his iPod's earphones into his ears. "LET'S RUNNNNN!"

He led. We followed.

I jogged with Darbie. We ran past Charlotte doing sit-ups in her school clothes. "Did you hear that?" I asked.

"Yeah. What do you mean, you're excited to run?" She tripped over her own feet and I braced her with my arm before she fell.

I said, "Not that. The blisters."

"Oh, *that*."

Charlotte's friend Misty interrupted us. "It just so happens that Charlotte's dad bought her the most amazing new cleats that cost, like, a hundred dollars. If shoes are even the slightest bit too snug, like brand-new cleats are sometimes before you break them in, they can give you blisters. It's not funny—in fact they are quite painful. You know they can get infected if they don't stay really clean?" Then she ran past us, catching up with the pack.

"You thinking what I'm thinking?" I asked Darbie.

"That depends on what you're thinking," Darbie said. Again, her left foot got in the way of the right one and she lost her balance. I gave her my hand so she didn't fall.

"What's your problem?" I asked.

"I don't know. I'm, like, uncontrollably clumsy."

I shook my head. "What I was saying was that I was thinking about the H-E-X."

Darbie thought about this. Her face told me that she was having trouble making out the letters I spelled.

"Hex," I said. "The Hexberry Pie. We gave her blisters."

"You know they can get infected?" Darbie mimicked Misty. "Man, hexes stink."

"Only for the one *being hexed*. As the *hexer*, I think they rock!" I said.

Darbie said, "And you're not worried we'll get what we deserve?"

"You worry too much," I told her.

With newfound energy I jogged my way up to Hannah and explained our good fortune.

Nine laps later Coach called, "GATHER AROUND, LADIES!" We all collapsed onto the grass. "Get some water," Coach said. He took a long pull on his own bottle and squeezed water onto his face. "You girls did really well today. I know the first few days of conditioning are hard. Eat a good dinner tonight. And get a good night's sleep." He took another drink. "Grab a colored mesh jersey; we'll scrimmage until your parents get here."

"I might puke," Darbie panted.

"NO CHITCHAT, GIRLS! Take your positions."

We jogged onto the field. Everyone was dog-tired,

except for Hannah. She easily dribbled down the field and scored.

Darbie dragged. The truth was, she wasn't looking so good at tryouts today and I was worried she might get cut from the team. That would totally stink. We had always been on the same team. I didn't know what was up with her—she was always a little clumsy, but not a total spaz like today, and yesterday on her Rollerblades.

Hannah must've thought the same thing, because she took the ball to the sideline for a throw-in, and on her way she nudged Darbie in front of the first white goal post. "Stay right here and get ready," she whispered.

With a grunt she tossed the ball long and high, right to Darbie's forehead. Darbie snapped her neck to hit the ball and made a perfect shot into the goal. Hannah might not have believed in the special powers of the Secret Recipe Book, but she was still a great pal to set Darbie up to look like a star—or at least not a total spaz.

"All right, O'Brien! That's what I'm talking about. Good job!" Coach clapped his hands.

I saw my mom arrive. She sat on the sideline talking to Mrs. Barney. I had a bad feeling about that.

At the end of practice we gathered our stuff by the bench. "How're those stomach muscles feeling?" Darbie asked Charlotte.

"My abs are like a rock." Charlotte patted her tummy.

"Unlike yours. You know, you're going to set a record as the fastest kid Coach has ever cut. Face it Darbie, you're going to be the first one cut from this team, and Kelly is going to lose the chili contest."

"No way." Darbie got in Charlotte's face. "Wanna take things up a notch?"

"Bring. It. On," Charlotte said.

"All right. If Kelly loses the chili contest, she has to rake your yard wearing whatever you choose. If she wins, you have to rake her yard wearing whatever *she* chooses."

Charlotte said, "You're. So. On." She and Misty walked off giggling.

I couldn't move my feet. I couldn't move my mouth. And thankfully, I couldn't move my arms. Because if I could, I would've run after Charlotte and taken back the bet. And I'd have whacked Darbie in the head for upping the ante *on my behalf!*

That's just wrong.

I managed to heave myself and all of my belongings into the minivan. Darbie and Hannah did the same.

Mom said, "You girls don't look so good."

We just sort of grunted.

"If you girls promise you'll still eat your dinners, you could talk me into buying you a little somethin' somethin' at Sam's," she said. She was trying too hard to be cool, but I was too tired to be embarrassed by her and I really needed the Swirley she was referring to. (I'm talking extra-thick.)

We nodded. Normally we would've whooped, but we were too beat.

She put the car in gear and drove toward Sam's. "By the way, Kelly, your father's and brother's voices came back. A little tea with my special honey drops did the trick. Mrs. Barney was telling me there's a virus going around. Oh, and Kell, when I was talking to her . . ."

Oh, no. Here it comes.

". . . She was telling me how badly Charlotte's feet hurt."

Yes!

"So, I offered for you to help take her books to school tomorrow."

And there it was. *Jab to the stomach,* as my father would say, and he knows what he's talking about, because he watches a lot of boxing.

"You've got to be kidding. Why? Oh, why, *why*?"

"Don't be so dramatic. It's only for a few days. And you're going to the same place as Charlotte. It's not a big deal."

I had really enjoyed the hex and seeing Charlotte do sit-ups for an hour. But now I had to help her? Maybe it was the curse—maybe that's what I deserved for hexing her legs and enjoying it so much: Death by Humiliation.

Sam delivered Swirleys to our table because we were too tired to walk over to the counter to get them. He even opened the straw for Darbie and bent it to her lips. She slurped, swallowed, and sighed. "Good stuff. Thanks, Sam."

When Mom went to Cup O' Joes, I said, "With the exception of having to help Charlotte with her books, the whole blister thing is exciting, doncha think?"

Darbie held a blank expression. "This is my excited face today," she said.

Hannah said, "I know what you're thinking, that somehow with that book, we caused Bud to lose his voice and Charlotte to get terrible blisters, but there are rational explanations for why those things happened. I don't think our Charlotte experiment proved anything. It could still be coincidental."

"If you ask me," I said, "two coincidences are two coincidences too many."

"We need more data," Hannah said.

"I'm game," I said.

Darbie couldn't pry her lips from around her straw. She just gave the "okay" sign.

My Swirley was so thick I couldn't suck it through the straw. I had to eat it with a spoon—but it totally hit the spot.

Hannah's Swirley was almost gone. She pushed all ten fingertips on her forehead so hard that they turned white.

"You did it again," I said.

She nodded. "Brain freeze. I can't help it, it's just so good."

12

Strife

Later that evening Mom called upstairs interrupting my homework. "That was Mrs. Silvers on the answering machine. Can you—"

"Let me guess. Scoop the poop," I said. I opened the Secret Recipe Book. That grouchy old dog-hater across the street was going to drive me to Crazytown if I didn't do something soon.

"Oh, and Kelly," Mom said, "when you go over can you—"

"Yes, I'll take her mail too. I'll go over in a few minutes." I remembered seeing something in the Book that I thought would be good for just such a situation. Ah, there it was, the FCS: Fresh Citrus Squeeze/For Causing Strife. This recipe had only four ingredients, so I could make it fast for a quick delivery. It called for crushed *menta*. I knew that was mint. We always had mint leaves in the spice cabinet. Mom and I use it in lots of different recipes.

Downstairs Mom was singing jazz and folding clean sheets in the laundry room, which was right next to the kitchen. "I'm going to squeeze an orange for the hag—err, I mean, Mrs. Silvers."

My mom looked at me through the doorway, a smile covering her face, "You're squeezing orange juice for Mrs. Silvers?" she confirmed in disbelief.

"Yeah. I started thinking that maybe if I'm nice to her, she won't bother me so much. Maybe she'll call Charlotte to clean her yard."

Mom said, "That would make more sense if Charlotte had a dog."

In the kitchen I squeezed the juice of an orange into a glass. "Not really. We both know that Rosey isn't the dog pooping in her yard. She only did once and that was a long time ago. But because of that, I'm singlehandedly scooping poop for any random dog who comes by and squats. It's only fair Charlotte should have the same opportunity."

"Speaking of Charlotte, since you're in a forgiving

mood, why don't you kiss and make up with her, too?"

Let's not get carried away. "Mom, I can name that tune in one note . . . NOT!"

Mom snapped a pillowcase as she shook it out.

I crushed a mint leaf under the base of a metal spoon.

Mom's head was halfway in the dryer. "What you're doing is nice. Maybe when you're old, someone nice will help you."

I sprinkled in a half pinch of crushed mint into the pulpy juice as I stirred.

I plopped a few ice cubes into the fresh citrus orange-mint-squeeze, grabbed the scooper, and headed across the street.

Knock-knock.

"Hi," I said cheerfully as the door opened a crack. "I'm going to clean up your yard. I also brought over your mail and some fresh juice for you."

A wrinkled hand came out and took the glass, and the door banged shut in my face. Not a word from that mean old woman.

Mission complete, as my dad says.

While I scooped poop for what I hoped was the last time, Darbie's words dangled in the back of my brain, "BEEEEWAAARRRREEE, MooHaHaHah!"

* * *

During my hot shower, I thought about Bud's voice and Charlotte's blisters and Hannah's need for additional experimentation. Back in my bedroom, I looked through the Book. There was one recipe that continually captured my attention. I e-mailed Darbie.

To: DarbieSk8s
From: KellyQCooker
>> D, I was thinking about another experiment . . . a love potion. —K

To: KellyQCooker
From: DarbieSk8s
>> K, Who and who? —D

To: DarbieSk8s
From: KellyQCooker
>> D, HH and FR. —K

To: KellyQCooker
From: DarbieSk8s
>> K, Darbie likey. —D

To: DarbieSk8s
From: KellyQCooker
>> D, Me 2. C U 2morrow. —KQ out

On my way to bed, I sniffed. I couldn't believe it. It was nine thirty and I smelled chili. I went downstairs. "Mom, what are you doing?"

Next to her was the Mammoth. The Mammoth was the biggest cup of the strongest coffee Cup O' Joe makes. "I'm glad you're here," she said frantically. "I made several small batches of chili to try out some different spice combos. I'd like you to test each one and tell me what you think. I have my favorite, but let's see what you think." She slid a spoon in front of me. "Try this."

I tasted it. "Water!" I yelled. OMG, it was so spicy!

She got me a glass. "Too hot? Is it too hot? I thought it might be too hot."

I nodded.

"Try this one." Mom shoved another spoonful of chili under my nose.

After the last one, I wasn't too psyched, but I took an itty-bitty taste. It was so smoky it made me cough. I drank the water again, choking on it as it struggled to get down my throat.

"Too much BBQ? I thought there might be too much BBQ," she said.

I nodded as I chugged more water.

Then she gave me a third spoonful. She looked at me like she was simply dying to hear what I thought. Reluctantly, I tasted it.

It was not immediately offensive, which was good. It was chunky with both meat and beans. I liked the balance of hot red pepper and cumin. There was a little sweetness that was interesting. But then there was a kicker that I couldn't identify. It was very pleasing, and while I couldn't put my finger on what it was, it reminded me of Thanksgiving and Christmas, and it made me feel happy. I tilted my head and thought about it. I still didn't know what it was. "Mom, this is so, so, so good. What is that flavor?"

"AHA!" she yelled. "I knew it. I knew you'd love it. I knew it, I knew it, I knew it."

"What's in it?"

She held up a regular old ordinary spice bottle that had been in our cabinet forever. Who would've ever thought that the spice of homemade apple sauce and pumpkin pie would go so well in chili?

Our annual Alfred Nobel School Chili Cook-Off secret weapon? Nutmeg.

13

Shade-Grown Ginseng

Question: *What weighs more, one hundred
pounds of flour, or one hundred pounds of nutmeg?*

Answer: *Charlotte's red canvas LL Bean backpack on the
morning I'm carrying it to school.*

The next morning there was a knock at the back
door. I saw blond hair.

Let the humiliation begin. I hoisted her backpack
over my shoulders and carried mine in front of my body.

On the bus in front of everyone, including Frankie and
Tony, Charlotte made a big deal about me carrying her
stuff.

She said, "Oh, Kelly, can you put it there?" She turned
to Misty. "It's just like having a butler."

Misty asked, "Do you tip her?"

"Do you tip a butler?" Charlotte asked.

I tuned out the rest of the conversation, which was peppered with giggles.

It was the ultimate humiliation that blurred the rest of my day like chocolate fudge in a Swirley. I didn't pay attention in any of my classes and I didn't eat my lunch. I did notice, however, that Darbie still had trouble with her foot coordination, holding her pencil in her hand, and keeping her books in her arms. She had an überbad case of the clumsies.

The backpack thing had me so livid, I only spoke to the girls long enough to tell them that I'd "dealt with" Mrs. Silvers, and arranged for them to come over after school. I told them not to come over right away, because I needed to run an errand. They agreed, and by the end of seventh period they stopped trying to make me feel better.

Charlotte didn't say anything, not even "thank you," when I delivered her backpack filled with cement at her back door. "If you think this is bad, just wait until you're raking my yard," the voice of genuine wickedness called to me as I walked off in a huff.

When I got home, Mom was working on a jigsaw puzzle on the dining room table. She looked at my expression. "Bad day?" she asked.

I nodded.

"What happened?"

"Charlotte happened."

"I'm sorry, honey."

I ignored her because "you should be" was the only thing I could think of to say.

"Mom, the club is coming over and I need something for the recipe we're going to make. I don't feel like walking down to La Cocina. Can you take me?"

She glanced at her watch. "Sure, sweetheart. Hey, how about staying up late with me to mass produce our chili?"

Staying up late cooking with Mom? That changed my mood and put a smile on my face. It reminded me of the reasons I loved cooking. She and I alone in the kitchen, just talking and stirring.

"Maybe I'll get myself a Mammoth." She snatched her purse. "And I'm thinking of pizza for dinner so we can start early on the chili."

"That sounds good," I said.

Cup O' Joe was noisy and crowded. "How about a hot chocolate?" she asked, ruffling my hair.

"That would be great." I pulled an ANtS sweatshirt over my head. "I'm going next door to get the stuff for the club."

"Don't you mean *secret* cooking club?"

I rolled my eyes. "Yes, that's the one." After I turned around, the corners of my lips curled up. I would've never admitted it to her, but sometimes she was actually funny.

I pushed open the door of Cup O' Joe and found the target of the love potion on the other side.

Enter Frankie Rusamano: "Whoa, where's the fire?" I was so close to him that I could smell his soap.

"Oops, sorry Frankie."

"You don't know your own strength. Maybe you should go out for the football team." He gently punched my arm.

My mom waved to Frankie. "Hi, Frankie, how's your family?" She inched up in line.

"Everyone's good. Tony and my dad are working on a landscaping project at the Rossis'. I'm heading there now. My mom's at home making sauce," Frankie replied over the bustle.

Mom asked, "Is she entering the Chili Cook-Off?"

"She wouldn't miss it," Frankie said. "She wants that chili pepper necklace for another year."

"Well, tell her I said hello and that we need to get together one of these days."

"Will do, Mrs. Q."

My mom was almost to the front of the line. "Frankie, do you want hot chocolate too?"

"That'd be great, Mrs. Q." He gave her a big grin that revealed his dimples.

He turned to me. "Sweet! That's what I came in for."

"I was about to go next door," I said to him.

He held the door for me and, to my surprise, Frankie followed me to La Cocina.

The shells hanging on the door knocked together as we

entered the Mexican cooking store. It felt like a museum that was closed for the night, or maybe one that had been deserted for years. Animals stared at each other. Sunlight was scarce. The smell of stale nachos floated in the air. Stacks of burlap-style cloth with colored zigzag patterns were piled on tables and stools.

Standing on a faded braided rug, Frankie mumbled, "Creeeeeepy." He examined each animal head. "I've been to Sam's and Cup O' Joe a zillion times and I can honestly say I've never been in here. Now I know why."

I found the spice rack holding corked bottles of various shapes, shades, and sizes, and using the alphabetical organizing system, I found the one I wanted filed under *G*: shade-grown Mexican ginseng. Scratchy black writing on a price tag read $10.95.

Frankie saw the tag over my shoulder. "Holy Stromboli, that's expensive for some dust."

"It's a spice that's hard to find, not dust. But it is expensive. I don't think I have enough money to pay for it."

"I have the money I was going to use for the hot chocolate, if you need it." He reached into the pocket of his cargo pants and found a crumpled five-dollar bill.

"Thanks, I'll pay you back," I said gratefully.

Frankie was a nice guy. I felt kind of bad borrowing money to buy something to use in a potion intended for him.

"It must be nice having a job," I said, counting the money in my hand. When I looked up, I suddenly saw that Señora Perez was inches from my face.

"*Buenos días*," she said slowly with her arms crossed over her chest. Wearing a thin bathrobe and slippers, she looked like she had just rolled out of bed. She checked Frankie out from head to toe, expressionless.

I felt the need to fill the quietness. "Ahhh . . . I . . . I'd like to buy this."

Señora Perez finished her visual examination of Frankie, took the bottle without looking at it, and walked to the back of the store. She disappeared through the curtain of colorful beads—red, gold, and green. I waited at an ancient cash register.

Frankie walked up behind me. "Maybe you were supposed to follow her back there?" He nodded toward the beaded doorway.

"I hope not," I said hesitantly.

"What? You look scared. Kelly Quinn is afraid of an old lady? She's shorter than my eight-year-old cousin."

"Shhh," I said. "I am not scared."

I gazed at the artwork while we waited. There were lots of dusty, framed photos of a beach that went on for miles before melting into choppy mountains rich with green plants. If I squinted, I could make out little homes, or huts or something, on the tops of the mountains.

Señora Perez emerged from the waterfall of shiny beads with her glasses hanging on an elaborate strand of jewels. She lifted the chain over her messy bun that reminded me of a Black and White Super Swirley. The hairdo gave the illusion that she was taller than she really was.

She perched the glasses on the tip of her nose. *"Diez, niña,"* she said, and turned the bottle in her hand to look at the name of the spice. Her eyes peeped over the rims of her glasses. She gave me a quizzical look. Then she looked at Frankie Rusamano, and back to me. *Why is she smirking?*

"Shade-grown ginseng, ah?" she asked.

I nodded and slid the wad of dollars and change across the counter. "Yes, it's for . . . for . . . a lemon smoothie." I think I started sweating.

She slid the money toward her very slowly. "A smoothie?" She looked at me as though she could read my thoughts. I swear that the look on her face said, *I know you're making a love potion for the kid standing right next to you, and are you sure you want to do that?*

Maybe I was being paranoid, but it was definitely getting hot in there.

Señora Perez pushed the buttons on the antique cash register. As though the sound of the keys dinging summoned a mythical flying creature, a black bird with a long beak shot through the beaded curtain and landed on the woman's shoulder.

I gasped in surprise and fear. But then I tilted my head, noticing something peculiar. Señora Perez had a wide, warped nose. The bird had a wide, warped beak. Señora Perez had disheveled hair. The bird had unkempt, mangy feathers. Looking at the bird and Señora Perez, I had a bizarre thought. Those two looked alike. Well, as much as a bird and a person *could* look alike.

Either Frankie was afraid of them, or shocked by the weirdness of their appearance, because the color drained from his face.

Señora Perez took my money and put the bottle in a small paper bag. I couldn't wait to get that bag and get out of there. Part of me feared that when I turned around, the door would be blocked by a dragon, and the animals on the wall would come to life and try to eat me. Or this creepy woman would trap me in a cage with her bird before feeding me to her pet iguana that lived in the basement.

Señora Perez didn't seem to notice the bird. She seemed more interested in staring at us.

"Gracias," I said. I saw my mother outside thumbing through the newspaper. No dragons, no iguanas, and no wall animals came to life.

When I was just two feet from the door, Señora Perez called to me. "You remember what I tell you, *Quien siembra vientos recoge temtestades?*"

There it was again.

* * *

Darbie and Hannah had already made themselves at home in my kitchen.

"What's with the sneakers?" I asked Darbie, who was without her signature blades.

"My mom took my skates away until I can stop being klutzy."

"That could take years," Hannah teased.

"Very funny, Hannah Haha," Darbie replied. "So, what are we making today?"

"I found a recipe for Bug Juice."

"Oh, no," Hannah said. "I can name that tune in two notes . . . no way! You're getting carried away, Kelly Quinn. I'm not drinking bugs. I'm not eating bugs."

"I have no problems with bugs, but we're not *actually* drinking them, are we, Kelly?" Darbie asked. "Because I'm with Hannah on this one. No. Eating. Bugs."

"Yes, I collected them last night after midnight. We need to squeeze their blood out—or we can put them in the blender."

Hannah said, "Seriously, I draw the line at eating or drinking any form of insect."

I *tisk*ed with my tongue. "Oh, I'm just joking with you guys. Do you really think *I* would drink bugs?"

We all chuckled.

"Really, what are we making today?" Hannah asked.

I said, "I want to know for sure whether the recipes in this book are special potions. It's time to put the Secret Recipe Book to the test with a *serious* experiment."

"What experiment?" Hannah asked.

"Go ahead, Kelly-Belly, tell her," Darbie said.

I hesitated. I was not sure how Hannah would react to being part of the experiment.

"WHAT experiment?" Hannah asked again.

"Hannah, don't say no right away." I opened my arms to my sides. "Open your mind, and let's just suppose for a minute that the secret recipes can make things happen."

"All right, I'm supposing," she said, but she blew her bangs out of her face.

I glanced at Darbie, indicating she and I were in this scheme together. "Do you still like Frankie Rusamano?"

"Duh. Of course." Hannah blushed.

My lips began to twist up. "Well, I was thinking . . ."

"About what?"

I enthusiastically spat it out. "A love potion."

"You can't be serious," Hannah said.

Darbie chimed in, as excited as me. "Totally, Shoobedoobedoowhop."

Hannah said, "I thought you were worried about a curse."

"It's worth the risk," Darbie said.

"I agree," I said. "I was thinking we could make this Bug

Juice—actually it's called Love Bug Juice—for Frankie and take it to him at work," I said. "He's working at the Rossis' house today."

Hannah tilted her head and considered this.

"What's the worst that could happen?" I asked. "If the potion isn't real, what do you have to lose?"

Hannah thought for another second. "And I could prove to you guys that this is all a bunch of baloney and we can start cooking regular stuff?"

Darbie and I nodded.

"Okay, my mind is certainly open to scientific experiment. Let's give it a try," said Hannah.

14

Hubba, Hubba

Darbie, Hannah, and I made a love potion for
Frankie Rusamano.

Although we'd been an official secret cooking
club for only a few days, we worked like an experienced
team of TV chefs.

I got a tall pitcher from my cabinet and poured in
chilled cranberry juice.

Hannah peeled and diced green grapes. Darbie sliced
a kiwi fruit. I mashed a jar of maraschino cherries. Each
fruit got plunked into the pitcher. Gradually the liquid
became a blend of rich colors.

I took the shade-grown Mexican ginseng out of my pocket and gave the petite green-tinted bottle to Hannah. She showered contents of the pitcher with the spice.

After plopping in generous amounts of ice cubes, it was done.

"It's beautiful," Darbie said, staring at the swirling juice.

"Should we go to the Rossis'?" I asked.

"I want to fix my hair," Hannah said.

Darbie said, "And I need to borrow something in your garage."

"Okay. I'll look for a Thermos." We all went in our own directions.

When I returned to the kitchen with the Thermos, I found droplets of Love Bug Juice on the kitchen counter and the floor.

BUD!

Thankfully, I saw there was still plenty of juice left for Frankie. In fact, it didn't all fit in the Thermos. So I resisted the urge to flatten Bud like an ant.

A second later Hannah called, "You ready?"

Through the front window I saw Darbie at the end of my driveway standing on my skateboard, which she'd borrowed from my garage. For some reason, I didn't have a good feeling about Darbie on my skateboard. I didn't want her to get hurt on my watch. But I didn't think she'd like me to suggest that she walk, so I went with it. "Ready," I said.

In lieu of falling, Darbie quick-stepped off the skateboard several times. I held the Thermos and told her she couldn't fall into me. She grabbed on to Hannah a few times to steady herself.

It didn't take long for us to spy the Rusamano Landscaping truck a few streets down. Frankie was spreading mulch. The back of his shirt was wet with sweat.

He lifted his head and staggered over to us. "Hi guys, I mean, girls. What up?"

For once, Hannah was at a loss for words.

I said, "We were just going for a walk."

"Hot today, huh?" Darbie asked, one foot on the skateboard.

"Sure is," Frankie looked at her strangely. "No soccer tryouts?" His face was flushed and it looked like he was getting sunburned.

I said, "Not today." I gently nudged Hannah with my elbow.

She managed to ask, "Uhh . . . are you thirsty?"

Frankie wiped sweat off his forehead. "Do I look thirsty?"

"Yeah . . . ," Hannah said. Her mouth clearly wasn't working right.

"We made Bug Juice," I said.

He hesitated. "Whoa, I'm not thirsty enough to drink bugs."

This made Hannah smile, but she was still too nervous to talk.

Darbie filled in the conversation. "It's not actually insects. It's cold and sweet, very yum-o-licious."

"Well, in that case."

Hannah still held the Thermos close to her. I gently bumped her arm, guiding the Thermos closer to Frankie's hand. Just then Tony, Frankie's twin brother, walked over, iPod buds buried in his ears.

It was odd how Frankie and Tony could look so much alike and so different at the same time. In a word, Tony was sloppy. His hair was mussed and needed a cut. And he slouched, hiding the fact that he was about a head taller than Frankie. Teachers always told him to pull up his pants. Frankie, on the other hand, kept his hair buzzed short and even now, working outside, it seemed he'd made some effort to tuck in his dirty T-shirt.

Frankie was the life of the party, whereas Tony kept to himself. I didn't really even know him. But here he came. He reached over Frankie's shoulder, took the Thermos, and chugged a big gulp before Frankie playfully elbowed him in the stomach. "Get your own, dude."

Tony returned the affection by making an armpit fart in Frankie's ear before jogging over to the landscaping truck.

"Real mature!" Frankie called, but Tony didn't seem to hear him.

At the truck, Tony ducked his head under the spigot of a cooler, letting water flow into his mouth, onto his face, and into his hair.

Meanwhile, Frankie put the silver rim of my dad's camping Thermos to his lips. He drank. "Wow. You were right, it's sweet." He looked right at Hannah and took another sip. "Why do you call it Bug Juice?"

Her mouth decided to work. "Ahh, umm, it's an opposite thing. You know, like the baseball player who pitches with his right hand and they call him 'Lefty,'" she said. "Or the shortest kid that people call 'Stretch,' or you call the chubby guy 'Slim,' or—"

Now maybe her mouth was working a little too much. I discreetly stepped on her foot and she closed her lips.

Frankie finished her thought. "So, you call the sweetest drink Bug Juice. It's weird, but I get it."

"FRANKIE!" His dad called over the growl of a chain saw. "Coffee hour is *finito*, back to work!"

"The boss," Frankie said with a nod. "Gotta go." He handed the Thermos back to Hannah. "Thanks, guys, I mean, girls."

"Honey! Dinner's getting cold!" Mom called out the back door to my dad, who was examining the tree in the Barneys' yard.

"It's a nice night, huh?" Dad asked when he came in.

I took my seat next to Bud and put my napkin on my lap. When I looked up, I saw my dad had poured the rest of the Bug Juice out of the Thermos and into a glass. He took a sip.

Ruh-roh.

My mom pulled the pizza slices onto plates. Dad hugged her. "That drink was scrumptious," he said.

"Oh, I didn't make that, Kelly and her friends did." Mom took a drink of the juice too.

Double ruh-roh.

"Well, it's yum-o-licious, as Darbie would say." He sat down, smacking his lips. "Looks like the cooking club is rockin' and rollin'."

Mom laughed. "*Secret* cooking club," she corrected.

I ignored her. "It's going well," I said cautiously, watching for my parents' reaction to the love potion. Actually, I'd forgotten that Bud drank some too. It seemed like I was the only one at the table who *hadn't* tried the Love Bug Juice.

I carefully surveyed the three of them. They looked normal. Well, as normal as my family could look.

"Remind me, who's in this club? Dad asked.

"Darbie and Hannah," I said.

Bud lifted his eyebrows up and down. "Hannah. Hubba, hubba!"

Hubba hubba? Okay, totally scratch what I said about

normal. As creepy as my little brother usually was, I'd never heard him use the phrase "Hubba, hubba."

I was not the only one surprised by this comment. "What was that, mister?" Mom asked.

Bud took a big bite of the top triangle of his pizza. "Sthee thure is perrtie," he said with a mouth full of food.

I caught my dad trying to hide a laugh.

"You leave your sister's friends alone." Mom wiped Bud's mouth with a napkin.

"But she is pretty. And have you seen her play soccer? She's, like, the best one on the team," he added.

When Dad thought no one was looking, he winked at Bud.

After dinner my dad unbuttoned and rolled up his sleeves. He placed dirty dishes in the sink. Mom watched him. "Since when do you help in the kitchen?"

"You go relax," Dad said. "I'll clean up in here." But Mom didn't relax, she sang along with the jazz on the radio.

Confirmed. Things were definitely NOT normal.

I retrieved my backpack and observed my dad with his soapy hands. He wiggled his body to the music and sang, "Hubba, hubba."

I left the kitchen, then turned back. "Mom, did Mrs. Silvers call today?"

Mom giggled at Dad's horrible dancing. "No, she didn't. Maybe that orange juice did the trick."

"Maybe." I thought maybe I had more positive data with Mrs. Silvers.

Then she added, "Do you have some homework to do?"

I fled Crazytown and hid in the safety of my room, where I called Darbie.

I told her what happened with my family at dinner after they drank the Love Bug Juice.

"Your family has always been a little strange," Darbie said. "Let's wait and see what happens with Frank—oh crap! Ouch!" I heard the phone tumbling.

"What happened?" I asked. "Are you okay?"

Darbie came back on the line. "I fell off the side of my bed and hit my funny bone on the dresser. There's nothing funny about it."

"What's with you lately? You're like a falling disaster."

"I don't know, but it sucks."

"Try to be more careful, Shoobedoo," I said before we hung up.

Then I jumped on my bed to get my journal out of the ceiling tile. I turned back a few pages and reviewed the past couple of days. I studied the warnings and called 1-800-Hannah. "Hey, pal, it's me."

Hannah said, "Hey, Kell, what's up?"

"I wanted to double-check the translation of *Quien siembra vientos recoge temtestades.*"

"Like I said, it's some kind of old Spanish saying. Just a sec." I heard her flip through a book. "This year instead of getting you a cookbook for your birthday I'm getting you a Spanish/English dictionary. Then you won't have to call me every time you need to know a word," Hannah said.

"Sure, but I really like calling *you*," I said. "Besides, sayings like this are hard to find in a dictionary."

"I know. I have a list of phrases in this book. It means 'You reap what you sow.' That's what this book says."

"Great, only now I need a translator for the English version, too. What does that mean?"

"It's what I told you before, you get what you deserve," Hannah said. "Kind of like 'what you do comes back to you' or 'what comes around goes around.'"

Slowly, I said, "Or it *returns* to you." Maybe I was onto something. "Hold on." I set the phone down and flipped through the heavy pages pasted into the encyclopedia and looked for the slip of paper that had fallen out. "Hannah, remember the scrap of faded paper that flew out of the Book? It said, 'Remember to Beware of the Law of Returns.'"

"So what?"

I said, "Señora Perez said practically the same thing as what was written on that old note!"

"I guess," Hannah said. "That's weird."

"It's more than weird. It's *another* freaky coincidence. And you know my theory?"

"Don't remind me. 'There's no such thing as coincidence.' Look, I gotta go. I'm pooped—oops, sorry. I know poop is a touchy subject for you lately." There was a giggle in her voice.

Everybody wants to be a comedian, as my father would say. In Hannah's case, I liked it when she joked. It reminded me of the good ol' days when she used to be a lot more fun. Before she was so worried about how she looked, what she wore, or what she ate. I can't imagine worrying about so much stuff.

"Actually, I think the poop issue might be solved," I said. "No call from Silvers today."

I set my Spanish translating aside, went to the kitchen, and did some schoolwork, but it didn't take long for the sound of sizzling ground beef to fill the room. Little dots of hot grease jumped out and onto the stove top. I took my position and used a spatula to move the bits of meat around. When the meat was all brown, I drained off the fat and carefully scooped the beef into the pot with the rest of the chili ingredients.

Now that Mom and I had nailed down the recipe we were using for this year's chili contest, we moved into mass production mode. We needed to manufacture enough fantastic chili for everyone in town to have a taste.

Mom zipped around the kitchen, chopping onions faster than a food processor. "Maybe you can bring a little pot of this over to Mrs. Silvers," Mom said. "Since you and she are, like, buddies now."

"I don't know if I'd go that far, Mom."

"Well, there's no such thing as too much good karma."

"What's that?" I asked.

"What?"

"Good karma?"

Mom explained. "Karma is when you get what you give. So, if you do nice things for people, nice things happen to you. Likewise—"

"If you do something bad, something bad will come back to you?"

Mom said, "You said it."

Karma? Sounded like the Law of Returns and the *Quien siembra*-thingamabob.

I stirred and let out a mammoth yawn.

"I'll finish up here," Mom said. "Why don't you go to bed, honey."

I didn't argue.

Lying in bed with Rosey wrapped around my legs, I couldn't stop thinking. *If you do bad things, bad things will happen to you.*

This idea made me a little nervous, because maybe the girls and I made my little brother lose his voice, and maybe we gave Charlotte painful blisters on her feet. I mentally examined the last few days: Darbie had Rollerbladed to my house a million times, and this week she wiped out. In fact, she couldn't stop wiping out. And me, I had to carry Charlotte's books. But why hadn't anything bad happened to Hannah?

Before drifting off to sleep, I got out of bed and approached the computer. I googled "Law of Returns." The online dictionary defined it exactly as Señora Perez and Hannah had. And it sounded a lot like karma. After surfing around, I found some info I didn't like about karma. I read that it was a phrase used by witches. Some scholars even believed that the Salem Witch Trial hangings in 1692 were actually the Law of Returns punishing those witches with death. Suddenly, carrying Charlotte's books didn't sound so bad.

My eyelids felt heavy. After a while, I fell asleep at the computer and dreamed. . . . I was walking to the bus stop, but when I turned around, my house had disappeared. Charlotte was on my shoulders and she was very heavy. I saw Bud in the distance. Behind him was a group of Gypsy-people dancing barefoot. I felt hot air on my back and turned to see a dragon chasing me. I ran as fast as I could, but Charlotte got heavier with each step. I called to

Darbie, but my tongue was gone. I thought Coach Richards was yelling at me to do sit-ups.

I woke up sitting at the desk.

The clock read four a.m.

Kelly Quinn out.

15

Punked-Out-Pumped-Up-Poo-Poo-Potion

Get:
1 bad dream
20 bricks
1 case of the heebie-jeebies
1 love-potioned seventh-grade boy

Directions:
Whisk together in Home Ec class until
everything is completely mixed up.

The next morning her majesty knocked on the back
door.

I sighed and got my stuff for school.

Apparently Charlotte had chosen to bring bricks to
school, just to make sure I suffered. And of course she
couldn't even carry her own stupid red umbrella. Charlotte

was talking and talking about her cousin's wedding . . . a dress . . . *blah blah blah.*

I saw a woman about my mom's age in a tennis outfit strolling down Mrs. Silvers's driveway toward the newspaper. Ever since we've lived across the street from Mrs. Silvers, I've never seen another person at her house.

"Good morning, girls," the woman said cheerfully.

"Hello," I said. Charlotte kept walking and talking, not even noticing that I had stopped. "Umm, who are you?" I asked.

"I'm Joanne Silvers, Regina's daughter. I'm staying here while she's in the hospital."

"Did you say 'hospital'?"

"Kelly Quinn, if we miss the bus, you're going to be sorry," Charlotte yelled from the end of the block, hands on her hips.

Joanne said, "You better get going." And she disappeared into the house.

At that precise moment everything became clear. We had been warned, we hadn't listened, and now we were cursed.

If you do bad things, bad things will happen to you. I gave Mrs. Silvers the Fresh Citrus Squeeze to cause her strife, so that she would stop calling me to scoop her poop. And now she was in the HOSPITAL!

What will the payback be?

WHEN?

At the next curb I came to a full stop. I mean, I completely halted and carefully looked both ways for oncoming traffic. By the time I felt it was safe to cross, Charlotte was halfway across the street, still talking. At the corner I stood way back on the sidewalk, for fear the bus driver would lose control and the giant yellow school bus would run me over.

Could that be a bad enough punishment for *SENDING SOMEONE TO THE HOSPITAL?*

I sat on the bus, holding my breath until Darbie and Hannah got on.

I couldn't talk.

"What's the matter?" Darbie asked. "You look like you've seen a ghost."

I was totally tongue-tied. *That's it! I've swallowed my own tongue. I won't be able to talk ever again!*

Hannah dropped her lunch out of its paper sack and handed me the bag. "Here, breathe into this," she said. "Count to ten."

I counted really fast, one-two-three.

Darbie said, "Slow down, Shoobe."

The bag crinkled as it collapsed and filled back up. I took several breaths before I lowered the paper bag to my lap. My fingers searched the inside of my mouth. *Phew.* My tongue was there.

I quickly explained the Law of Returns, Señora Perez's warning, karma, and my late-night Internet research.

"They're all the same thing?" Darbie double-checked.

I nodded and told her the rest. "Remember last time Mrs. Silvers called me to scoop? Remember I told you that I'd just had it with her? I stirred up a drink from the Book."

Hannah said, "That doesn't sound so bad."

"I made a drink that would cause *strife*." I leaned my head forward onto the back of the green plastic bus seat.

"Wow, strife is not good," Darbie said. She stared out the window. "What exactly is strife?"

Hannah said, "If you want to cause someone strife, you want to cause them a difficulty or a hassle, maybe a conflict or problem of some kind."

"Sure," I said. "Hassle, difficulty, conflict. They're all fine. I just wanted her to leave me alone. And this morning I found out that she's in the hospital. Do you know what that means?"

"You poisoned her?" Darbie asked.

"Oh my God, do you think I poisoned her?"

Hannah said, "No. You didn't poison her. What did you put in the drink? Not drain cleaner or anything like that, right?"

"No," I said. "Just oranges, lemon juice, cherry juice, and mint, like the Book said."

"See," Hannah said. "You didn't poison anyone."

"Then there's *no problemo*," Darbie said.

I picked up the bag and started to breathe in it really fast again. Into it I said, "Yeth, therth thill—"

Hannah pulled the bag away. "We can't understand you. What's wrong?"

"There's still a big problem. I made her a drink from the Book, which sent her to THE HOSPITAL!" I exclaimed. "The warnings say that something bad is going to happen to *me* now."

Hannah tried to calm me. "She got sick. Old people go the hospital all the time. It just happened on the same night you brought her the juice. It's just a co—"

"Don't you dare say 'coincidence,'" I said.

Darbie said, "I have to agree with Kelly on this one, Hannah. You saw what happened to Bud and Charlotte. It can't all be a coincidence—those recipes from the Book have some special powers."

Hannah blew her bangs out of her face.

Darbie asked, "I mean, what are the odds of Mrs. Silvers going to the hospital *right after* Kelly gives her some punked-out-pumped-up-poo-poo-potion she made from an ancient book of hidden secret recipes that contained a warning saying 'Beware of the Law of Returns'?"

I answered: "Those odds are not very good. Not very good at all. But I really didn't mean to hurt her!"

"It appears that doesn't matter. We need to keep you

really safe," Darbie said. "OMG!" She clapped her hand over her mouth.

"What?" Hannah asked.

Darbie lowered her hand. "I just had a thought about this Law of Returns mumbo-jumbo-jigsaw-mambo. What if I got the klutzies for giving Bud that Shut-the-Heck-Up Cobbler? And . . ." She slapped her face again.

"What?" I asked.

"You're carrying Charlotte's books as payback for hexing her legs," she said. "Think about it. I was the one who added the vetivert to the cobbler, and you added the rue to the pie. "And . . ." She slapped her face a third time. This time her eyes got really wide.

"What now?" I asked.

"Hannah . . . ," she said, her face growing pale.

"What about me?" Hannah asked.

"What's going to happen to you for"—Darbie looked up the aisle and lowered her voice—"potioning FR with magic Love Bug Juice? You added the special ginseng."

We were so busy speculating about the disastrous fate that awaited Hannah that we didn't notice that the Rusamanos had gotten on the bus, or that the bus had arrived at school. None of us checked out Frankie's current love status.

I gathered my things and Charlotte's stuff. Hannah and I started to get off the bus. Darbie stopped us. "Let me go first. I need to make sure nothing bad happens to you two Shoobedoobedoowhops today. I can handle a few bruises." Darbie walked down the long bus aisle, inspecting every inch of the bus for danger. She descended down the first step. Then, tripping over her own feet, she plunged to the curb. Her backpack broke her fall.

Hannah blew her bangs out of her face. "And who's going to make sure nothing bad happens to *you*?"

"I'm all right!" she called from the ground.

I dropped Charlotte's hundred-ton backpack at her locker. As usual, she failed to thank me. We headed to homeroom. I told the girls about my dream on the way.

The teacher began calling roll: "Bill Applegate."

"Here."

"What should I do?" I asked Hannah.

"You should just chill out," she said. "I hate to state the obvious, but Darbie fell down because she isn't a great Rollerblader. Don't make this into something it isn't."

"Hannah Hernandez?"

"Here!" She lowered her voice. "If you really think that doing bad things gives you bad luck, why don't you try doing some good things to get some good luck?" She straightened her books on her desk. "I don't think you're in any danger, but if you think you are, there's someone you can go to for help."

Darbie said, "Don't say what I think you're going to say."

"Señora Perez."

"She said it anyway," Darbie said. "That lady gives me the heebie-jeebies."

"Darbie O'Brien?"

"Here."

Hannah said, "Fine. Don't talk to her. Kelly can become a tongue-tied, barefoot Gypsy who gets chased by a dragon instead."

I said, "Hannah's right. Señora Perez knows something about the Law of Returns. Maybe she even knows something about the Book. In the meantime, we need to think about how to undo this mess."

"Fine." Darbie sighed. "We'll go see Señora Perez."

"Kelly Quinn?"

"What do you mean *we*?" Hannah asked. "I like to keep a distance between myself and animal carcasses. Thanks anyway."

"What are you, chicken?" Darbie asked. She put her hands under her armpits and moved her elbows up and down. "Boc, boc, boc."

Hannah said, "Sticks and stones, Darb, sticks and stones."

"MISS QUINN? Are you with us today?"

"*Sí!*"

* * *

Over the mixer's hum I heard Mr. Douglass clapping his hands. I turned it off and saw Frankie Rusamano standing at the front of the classroom. "Okay, class," Mr. Douglass said. "We have a new student to add to our class. Everyone, please welcome"—he looked at a pink slip of paper from the school office—"Franklin Rusamano to our happy haven of free expression. Franklin, you may choose to work with anyone you wish. And welcome!"

Frankie cautiously backed away from Mr. Douglass, dropped his books on an empty desk, and came over to my kitchen area.

"Hi, Franklin," I said. "Now who looks scared? Frankie Rusamano is scared of the Home Ec teacher."

"I'm not afraid of the teacher. I'm afraid of cooking. So I'm glad *you're* my partner."

Partner? "Don't you ever cook at home? Isn't that, like, your mom's favorite thing to do?"

"Exactly. She cooks. I eat. I'm not afraid of eating. I'm good at eating, actually." He peeked into the bowl and slipped his index finger along the edge for a lick. He tasted it and looked at me. "Mmmmm, good. I'm really glad you're my partner. You know, we don't spend enough time together."

"We don't?" *What's gotten into him?*

"No. I've been thinking. We should probably hang out more often." He cocked an eyebrow.

"We should?" *What is he talking about?* I turned the

mixer back on and blended nervously. Loudly I asked, "Umm, what are you doing here? I mean, why are you even in Home Ec?" I turned off the mixer.

He smiled, mouth closed. "Maybe it's just to spend more time with you."

Okay, something is wrong here. "Seriously?" I looked at Frankie like he was crazy.

"Sure. But I also forgot to sign up for a non-core class this year. The guidance counselor looked at my schedule and told me I would have to add one or make it up at summer school. I don't want to go to summer school. Woodworking, Drawing, Painting—even Pottery was full. So here I am. But I didn't realize you were in this class. Now it's not as bad as I thought." He did the eyebrow thing again. "Did you already find out if you made the soccer team?" Frankie asked.

"Not yet. We have two more tryouts."

"I heard that Coach is going to take everyone who tried out. But even if he didn't, you would still definitely make the team," he said, staring at me strangely. I wiped my cheek in case there was some flour on it.

"Gee, thanks for the vote of confidence. But, if that's true, then why would he bother having tryouts?"

"Probably because it makes you guys—I mean girls—practice harder."

"I don't think Coach Richards would do that," I said.

But, now that I was thinking about it, I didn't see why he couldn't take everyone. Only about eighteen girls were trying out. And I had to admit I'd been running my heart out trying to impress him. If Frankie was right, Coach Richards was quite clever.

"Do you wanna mix?" I asked.

"Not really. You're doing a great job." He stared at me with a twinkle in his eye.

Why is he looking at me like that? "Are you feeling okay?" I touched his forehead and suddenly jerked my arm away. "You shocked me!"

"What can I say? Maybe there's some kind of chemistry between us."

Okay, we've reached a level of weirdness that I'm not sure I can handle.

"You're in an awfully good mood," I told him, angling the muffin pan so I could pour in the batter.

"Why wouldn't I be in a good mood, here with you, watching you cook. You don't have a problem with me watching you cook, do you? I like watching you cook."

I shrugged as Mr. Douglass strolled over and looked over my shoulder. I poured the batter into muffin tins that Frankie now held. "Excellent. Franklin and Kelly, you make a wonderful team."

"See, Kell, I told you so," Frankie whispered to me, and then he did the craziest thing. . . . He winked at me.

OMG. Could the Bug Juice have backfired? That was it! The Love Bug Juice got its target mixed up. And now Frankie had the hots for me instead of Hannah!

Question: *What was I going to do?*

Answer: *I was going to visit a spooky Mexican cooking store to talk to a fortune-teller with a freaky lookalike bird and beg her to help me get out of this mess.*

With my muffins laid out on a cooling rack under Mr. Douglass' nostrils, I speed walked out of Home Ec to get away from Frankie. "You've done it again, Ms. Quinn," I heard Mr. Douglass say as I scooted out of the classroom.

I stopped Darbie in the hallway.

"Darbie, listen carefully, we only have a few minutes before Science, and my legs don't want to find out what Coach Richards will do if we're late."

"What's the matter?"

"There's a little problem with the Love Bug Juice."

"Oh no, please tell me Frankie hasn't turned into a grasshopper."

"No," I said.

"Moth?"

"No."

"Oh no, not a scorpion. It's a scorpion isn't it? Something venomous," Darbie said.

"No!" I held her arms to keep her attention. "Frankie has a crush on me. Maybe he's in love with me, who knows. At this point, anything is possible."

"Yeah, and I'm gaga over Mr. Douglass."

"You are?" I asked. This was a bigger mess than I thought.

"No. I was just kidding," Darbie said. "Get a grip."

"Please don't joke right now, Darb. I'm totally serious. We have to go to La Cocina *today*. The Law of Returns is gonna get me. Maybe I'll die a painful death. We need to reverse the Law of Returns *and* we need an antidote for the love potion before Hannah finds out about Frankie."

"Sounds like we're going to have a busy afternoon," she said. Darbie was such a great friend. "But I've had a crap-ola day too. I got gum in my hair. The nurse had to cut it out. Look." She showed me a section of her hair, but I didn't think it looked any different. "And I sat on my Twinkie. I look forward to my afternoon Twinkie. Today I didn't have one. So, I'm grumpy."

"Thanks for warning me." Frankie crushing on me certainly wasn't a good thing, but it didn't seem so awful compared to the bad luck Darbie was having.

Darbie declared, "We need to get rid of this bad luck before I wither away to nothing from lack of Twinkies."

"We will. This afternoon. At La Cocina."

Darbie said, "I might not last that long."

"Well, be careful. I'm going to avoid Frankie. And until we can talk to Señora Perez, let's just do as many nice things as we can in case Hannah is right about getting some good luck from it."

Just then Mrs. Eagle, the librarian with supersonic hearing, walked up and said, "Girrrls, the late bell has rrrung." (She rolled her *R*s when she talked.) "You arrre now late. So, you will spend the afterrrnoon with me in detention." She walked into the library and closed the door.

"Well, that's just hunky-flippin'-dory," Darbie said. "One more bad thing to add to my list. Detention. No, it's worse. Detention without a Twinkie."

"Well," I said, "so much for soccer tryouts today. Coach Richards is gonna love this.

16

Being Nice

I chased Billy Applegate. "Here, Billy, you dropped your pencil back there." I handed it to him, and held the door to the classroom open for him, and for a few others coming in.

As soon as I took my seat I realized I needed to go to the bathroom. I asked Coach for a hall pass, which he reluctantly gave me. "Hustle," he said.

In the bathroom I found Darbie, standing next to the sink and holding a stack of paper towels. She handed one to Misty after she'd washed her hands. "Good job washing," she said to Misty. "You can't put a price on killing germs."

Misty said, "You're a weirdo."

"You have yourself a nice, germ-free day," Darbie said to Misty's back.

"What are you doing?" I went into the stall.

"Being nice." She lowered her voice and whispered through the crack in the door. "Reversing the Law of You-Know-What."

"Misty's right. You are a weirdo."

"I don't see you coming up with any better ideas."

I finished in the stall, washed, and took a towel from Darbie's stack. "I will. Come on, we're late."

"I already have detention," she said, but she followed me in anyway.

I returned to my seat just in time for homework collection. I popped up and gathered everyone's papers. I neatly left them on Coach's desk. After class I pushed in everyone's chairs and erased the boards. Turning to be thanked by Coach for my niceness, I found that he'd left the room—and so had Darbie. I could hear Darbie in the hallway. "Be careful," she said. Don't slip. Wet floor."

"What now?" I asked her.

"I don't want anyone to fall and get hurt, so I'm diverting people from this spill to a safer traffic pattern. Isn't that nice?"

"I suppose." Maybe she'd come up with a good one.

"Move along, people," Darbie said, waving kids in a certain direction.

As the hall cleared, I picked her backpack up from against the wall. I noticed an empty water bottle in her pack. "Darbie," I said. "How did that puddle get there?"

She didn't look at me, but after the hall was clear, she bent down and wiped it up.

17

Bees

Darbie wasn't happy that I volunteered for us to shelve library books during detention. She just stuck them in the wrong places, sometimes not even bothering to look at the spine of the Book. About every ten minutes Hannah, all the other ANtS soccer hopefuls, and Coach Richards ran past the library window. Charlotte wasn't with them.

"Now we're never going to make the team," I said. "Coach Richards isn't going to take us after missing tryouts."

"You don't have anything to worry about. You're a good soccer player. I'm a total spaz."

"*Girrrls.* Therrre is no talking in detention."

When we were done shelving (silently), we sat (quietly) and did our homework (without a sound) until we were excused. We flew to the locker room and changed into our soccer clothes faster than the speed of light. We sprinted to the field for the last five minutes of practice. Coach looked at us running down the hill, an hour late, and just shook his head. A few steps before reaching the bottom, Darbie wiped out, rolling the last few feet. Thankfully, Coach didn't see that part.

Darbie whispered to me, "So much for balancing out the bad luck. What a load of crap. I shelved library books. Can you believe that? I'd rather push chopsticks under my toenails than shelve library books."

Coach called to us over his shoulder, without making eye contact. "Join Barney." Charlotte was doing stomach crunches. We crunched. After a dozen my belly burned. Charlotte must have been doing them for a long time now, because her face was Texas hot sauce red.

The girls were scrimmaging. Hannah dribbled around the defenders wearing yellow practice jerseys. She shot and scored. The ball rolled under the goal's net and into the bushes.

Hannah jogged into the bushes to retrieve it. Suddenly, she came out screaming.

"Ahh! Help!" She ran around the field waving her arms and crying.

Coach yelled, "Hannah, are you okay?"

"Ah! Bees! Help!" She ran to Coach Richards. "Coach, get 'em off me. Ouch! They're stinging me!" Coach Richards swiped the bees off with his clipboard and sprayed them with his water bottle. In a minute all the bees were gone. Coach Richards led her to the bleachers.

"Let me see those stings." He grabbed lotion out of the first aid kit and spread thick pink liquid all over Hannah. When Coach was done, Hannah looked like she had gotten into a fight with a Tootie Fruity Super Swirley and lost.

We met Hannah after practice as she was getting her backpack.

"You ready?" I asked.

"For what?" Hannah asked, wiping dirt off her hands.

"We're going to see Señora Perez."

"Oh, man. I really don't want to. I have homework to do," Hannah said. "And these stings really hurt. I just want to take a hot bath."

"Well, I *really* need to talk to her," I said. We hadn't told Hannah about Frankie. I figured that if I could reverse the Love Bug Juice potion, I wouldn't have to.

Darbie said, "It's the Law of Returns."

Hannah asked, "What is?"

"The bee stings. It's the return for giving Frankie a love potion. You were the one who added the ginseng. Now all three of us have been zapped by the Law of Returns."

Hannah had trouble heaving her backpack onto her back. She yelped when the canvas touched her tender skin. "Darbie, I never thought I'd say this, but I'm beginning to think maybe you're right. Maybe it is the Law of Returns."

"Speaking of Frankie," I said. "Have you seen him?"

"Nope. Not all day. So much for the experiment," Hannah said.

Darbie and I shared a glance.

"But"—Hannah pointed—"there goes Tony." Tony rode past the field on his bike. His neck twisted to see the soccer field as he passed by.

Hannah said, "Guys, I'm hot and hungry, and I'm just not in the mood to play Nancy Drew today."

Darbie said, "But we need to turn off these returns. Kelly can't carry Charlotte's books forever. And if I keep falling down, I'm going to break a bone. Maybe an important one. And you—do you want to continue to get stung by flying insects?"

"No," Hannah answered. "But does it have to be today?" She winced in pain.

"I have an idea," I said. "Why don't you walk down the street with us and you can go to Sam's. I'll even buy you a Swirley. And you can relax in the air-conditioning and do your homework while we go to La Cocina. Hopefully Señora Perez can explain how to undo the curse. Then we'll meet you when we're done. It won't take us long."

"Unless she turns us into frogs or something, in which case we'll need you to rescue us, if we can't hop away," Darbie said. "Consider yourself our backup."

Hannah blew her bangs out of her face. "Fine, but I'm getting a large Swirley."

We hoisted our backpacks onto our shoulders and walked five blocks to the strip mall. On the way, I tried to think how I could prove to Hannah that the Love Bug Juice experiment had worked. We had the data she was looking for, but if she found out that Frankie loved me instead of her, she'd be crushed, and I didn't want to do that to my BFF.

How was I going to do this?

When we arrived, Hannah wished us luck and offered to order our Swirleys. "The yuush?" Hannah asked. (Our speak for "the usual.")

It struck me that she was still dotted with pink bee-sting lotion. "Um, Han—"

Darbie interrupted, "Yes sirree, ma'am. Rocket Launching Rainbow. Extra chunky, *por favor.*"

"And a Black and White for me," I said. "But, Hannah—"

"Don't worry about me. I'll be fine here by myself. I have to read for History."

I figured what she didn't know wouldn't hurt her.

Sam certainly didn't care what she looked like, if he even noticed.

Upon our arrival at the door to La Cocina, Darbie said, "Let's chat with this kooky fortune-teller cat, find out how to reverse the Law of Returns, get an antidote for Frankie, and get the hex out of there, because I hear my Swirley calling me. Can you hear it? *Darbie, drink me. . . .*"

18

Balance

Fill a room with:
1 moose head
1 big buzzard
1 raccoon
1 deer head
1 rabbit
1 squirrel
Each of which was probably cute and cuddly in life.
But now they're crusty, neglected, and, well . . . dead.

Directions:
Stuff them all and give them bright, glass eyes. Hang them on your
walls until they give goose bumps to anyone who walks by.

The string of shells jingled, but no one came out from behind the mysterious beaded curtain. "Hello?" I called.

No one answered.

"Let's look around," I said.

"Oh, that sounds like great fun," Darbie said.

The overhead lights were out, but the room was filled with an eerie glow coming from lighted candles set on the counters and shelves, and thick pillar candles rested on the floor. They gave just enough brightness to illuminate a thick layer of dust and brought a glow to the glass eyes surrounding us. My mom would've had a festival cleaning the joint.

Darbie pointed to a candle that was close to the wall. "Fire hazard," she said. The scent of burning candles was overpowered by the aroma that came from the back of the store. Someone was cooking something familiar: chili.

I saw Darbie's shoulders quiver abruptly. "Oooh, I got a chill," she said.

Although the tinted windows made the sky outside appear extra gloomy, I couldn't miss the heavy black clouds looming. But I kept my focus on searching the shelves.

Behind a large rack of ponchos there was an armoire filled with small bottles of elixir. Darbie and I scanned them. "What are we looking for?" she asked.

"An antidote for Love Bug Juice, or something like that," I said. I picked up several little silver shaker bottles that sounded like they were filled with nuts or dried beans. "And I suppose we need enough for Charlotte's blisters."

"Do we have to?"

I said, "I think we do. We can't let her have funky blistered feet forever."

"Then you need something for Mrs. Silvers, too," Darbie said.

"Good point."

"That is, if she's still alive," Darbie said.

"That's very helpful, Darbie. Thanks for the positive attitude."

"No problem, Shoobe. That's what I'm here for." We looked around. Then Darbie said, "But Bud's voice came back on its own. That's weird, huh?"

A lightbulb went on in the cobwebbed section of my brain. *Can it be that simple?* I said, "Darb, you're a freakin' genius! I know what we need to get. I think I know what the antidote is."

I told her what to look for.

"Half this stuff is in Spanish," Darbie said. She was right. We really could've used Hannah's help.

We wandered around the store.

I examined the jars and tins on the bottom shelf. One of the jelly jars was filled with the most disgusting things that looked like tails and something that used to be spiders. *So gross!* Then I saw a shimmery golden tin with a familiar bee on it. The bee wore a sombrero. I picked up the tin and turned it over. There was something written in Spanish that I couldn't read, but it didn't matter. I remembered that the drops inside made Bud's voice come back. *Holy guaca-mole, I've found it!*

"Maybe we should just go find that Señora," Darbie said. "I have a date with a lonely Swirley that's melting."

I took the tin and Darbie didn't see me slide it into my pocket. "We're all set. I have a plan," I announced confidently.

Before Señora Perez could magically appear, we dashed toward the door. I stopped, turned, and ran back to the cash register. I pulled a handful of money out of my pocket. Without counting it, I slapped it onto the counter.

"*Gracias,*" Señora Perez said, sweeping the colorful beads aside.

We had almost made it.

"Remember what I told you?" Señora Perez asked.

"*Quien siembra* blah blah . . . ," Darbie said, totally annoyed that we hadn't made it to the sidewalk.

"*Si,*" Señora Perez replied.

I said, "It's the Law of Returns."

"That's right," Señora Perez said. "It has found you."

"Are you psychic?" Darbie asked.

"Oh no, not psychic. I can see the bruises on your legs, Darbie. And the worry on Kelly's face. And I saw the stings on your friend when she walked by. I see the Law of Returns has found you, as I thought it might."

"Then it's real?" I asked.

"I can assure you that the Law of Returns is very real. You see, the universe must always be in balance. If you do something bad, something bad will come back to you. Maybe not right away, but it will come. I promise you."

"But how do we stop it? There must be a potion or something that can undo it, right?"

"There is no potion than can restore the balance of the universe. But you can take matters into your own hands and restore balance on your own before the fates of the Law of Return do it for you."

"So we can create the equal and opposite reaction before nature does it for us?" I asked. Hannah would've been proud of me for thinking so scientifically.

Darbie looked at me like I was a possessed Twinkie.

"*Si*," said Señora Perez.

"For example, we could do something good to balance something bad?" I confirmed.

"I see," Darbie said. "We help an old lady cross the road, and bada-bing, no Return. Right? Well, I've been doing nice stuff all day, and no bada-bing."

"Good deeds aren't as simple as 'bada-bing,'" Señora Perez said evenly. "They take some effort, some heart." She pointed to her chest when she said "heart." "You must really mean it, or it won't work."

"But what *will* work?" Darbie asked.

"That," Señora Perez said, "is for you to figure out."

19

Moon Honey

"So, we have to be nice again?" Darbie asked.

"Like, really nice," I replied. "Nicer than at school."

She rubbed her temples. "I'm getting a headache. So, what's this plan of yours?"

I put thoughts of kindness aside. "We need to get Frankie down here. He'll confess his love to me in front of Hannah, which will convince her the Secret Recipe Book is full of special potions. Then I'll give him one of these." I took the tin out of my pocket and shook it. "And I think it will reverse the potion."

"Sounds good to me," she said. "Except how do you intend to get Romeo to Sam's?"

Suddenly, the door to Cup O' Joe swung open and out came Mrs. Rusamano carrying a short, steaming cup.

The timing of Mrs. R. standing right there in front of us exactly when I needed her gave me goose bumps.

"Weird," Darbie muttered. "You've been hanging around that Señora too long, if you can make something like that happen."

I said, "Hi there, Mrs. R."

Then the door to Sam's swung open and Hannah came out. "There you are," she said. "I was getting worried. Your Swirleys are melting."

Mrs. R. said, "Hello, girls." She looked at each of us and stopped at Hannah. I assumed she was going to say something about the pink blobs of lotion on her skin, but instead she said, "You look thin. Are you eating enough?"

"Sure. It's soccer season, you know. I run a lot."

"I just made some cannoli. I'll send some with Frankie to school Monday."

"Really?" I asked. "Boy, do I love cannoli! It's my favorite. That sounds great, doesn't it, Darbie?"

I elbowed Darbie, encouraging her to agree with me. "Yeah, it's my fav," she said.

"You'll love it. It's Tony's favorite, next to my tiramisu," said Mrs. R.

"Oh wow, I can't wait until tomorrow," I said. "You've got my mouth watering."

"I've got an idea," she said. "Why don't I call Frankie and ask him to bring it down here right now?"

Perfect. "Grea—"

Hannah interrupted me. "That's not really necessary. It can wait until tomorrow."

"Nonsense, it's no trouble. Besides, I'm sure he'd love to see you," said Mrs. R. I wasn't sure who she was referring to when she said that. I think it was me, but I didn't make a big deal out of it.

Mrs. R. continued. "I'll call him from the car. I've got to go, I'm late for church." She dug for her keys and surveyed the sky that was growing dark both from dusk and clouds. "Looks like rain, you'd better get inside." When she got in her car and secured her double espresso in a cup holder, she picked up her rhinestone-clad cell phone and talked while she backed out of the parking lot.

"What the heck did you do that for?" Hannah asked.

I opened my palms, like I didn't know what she was talking about. "What?" I walked into Sam's and the girls followed.

Our Swirleys were on the table waiting for us.

"Come to mama," Darbie said to her Swirley glass. She took a sip of the top layer. "Ahhh." She looked like she'd floated off to heaven. "Good Swirley." She patted the glass like it was a puppy dog.

Hannah said, "Tell me what happened."

I took the tin out of my pocket and showed her.

"That's an antidote?" Hannah asked.

"I'm pretty sure."

"It doesn't look like anything special," Hannah said.

"I've seen this before." I explained how the tin looked familiar, how its contents helped with Bud's and Dad's throats, and how my mom claimed it cured anything.

Hannah took the tin and translated the writing on the bottom: "'Mexican Moon Honey. Gathered from Cedronian bees the morning after the full moon. Full moon beams have the power to mend wrongdoing.'"

Darbie said, "That sounds like an antidote to me. Good job."

"What's 'Cedronian'?" I asked.

"A certain breed of bees, I guess," Hannah said. "I'm not a bee expert."

We looked at her and laughed. She joined us. "Except for bee stings, of course," she added.

Hannah sucked in a big sip of her chocolaty drink and grabbed the bridge of her nose. "Ah! Brain freeze!" She pushed her palm out, signaling for us not to talk. She switched to the one-minute finger, then opened her eyes. "Okay. It's better now."

Darbie asked, "Why do you always do that? You know it hurts your head, but you slurp really fast anyway."

"I can't help myself. Maybe that's why the Swirley is called Death by Chocolate . . . you die from a frozen brain."

Suddenly a cool breeze slipped through the door—along with Frankie Rusamano and a cardboard box that I guessed contained cannoli.

Immediately the sight of him made me nervous. I hadn't told Hannah about Frankie being in love with me. I hoped he wouldn't swoon over me—she'd be so bummed.

He waved cautiously, like we'd made him self-conscious. "Hi, guys," he said. "I mean, girls. I heard there was a pastry emergency and I had to come right down. What's up?" He did a double-take when he saw the goop on Hannah's face, but quickly and politely averted his gaze to the rows of ice cream. I was so used to looking at her by now, I'd forgotten to remind her about the lotion.

He slid a chair over to the table and sat between me and Hannah. Surveying our tall, frosty glasses, he picked up Hannah's and took a sip. "Mmm. Chocolate. My favorite. Hey, Sam," he called. "Can I have one of these, please?" He rested his elbows on the table. "So, my mom says you needed cannoli right now. She says Hannah is too skinny and why didn't I tell her that sooner." He set the box on the table, all the while looking at Hannah. "There's a tiramisu in there too. Tony thought you liked tiramisu, Kell."

"I do. But I didn't know he knew that."

Sam yelled over, "You're all set, Frank-o."

I was closer to the counter. "I'll get it." I went to the counter and picked up the freezing brown Swirley. It was my chance to reverse the Love Bug Juice.

With my back to my friends and Sam busy wiping down the counter, I slipped a square of crystallized Moon Honey into the glass. I took a long spoon and stirred. I imagined the Swirley was going to bubble and steam like a brew in a cauldron, but the crystal just dissolved.

I gave the Swirley to Frankie along with a straw, which he depapered, slid in, and took a long pull from.

Frankie held up his hand, closed his eyes, and winced.

OMG, I've poisoned him!

20

Brain Freeze

Freeze:
Ice cream in large quantities
Chocolate and other candy
Cream

Direction:
Mix it all together and suck as hard and as fast as you
can until you numb the front third of your brain.
Continue until it causes extreme pain.

"Sorry, brain freeze." Frankie grabbed his head. "Oh! Man, that hurts." He remained like this for a few seconds. "But I can't help myself. It's so good."

Hannah smiled.

"How do you feel?" I asked. Darbie looked at me questioningly. I nodded—yes, I'd given him the honey. We watched carefully for his expression as he replied.

"Fine. Why?"

"Just wondering," I said. There was no sign that he was in love with me.

Looks like the Moon Honey did its thing.

We continued staring at him, waiting for some kind of reaction. "What?" He looked at his shirt. "Did I spill?" He wiped his nose. "Booger?"

Hannah looked from person to person like there was something going on that she didn't know about, which there was.

"Who do you love?" asked Darbie, always the subtle lady.

"What?" he shouted.

"Just making conversation." She casually examined her cuticle.

"Come on. What gives? I already think you guys, ah, girls, are nutso. Believe me. Nothing you tell me is going to change that."

There was silence, which I felt compelled to break. "We're having a disagreement."

I explained to Frankie about the Secret Recipe Book, the potions, and how strange things had started to occur. I didn't know how good it would feel to put it into words. At first the girls seemed hesitant, but soon they joined me, and I couldn't get a word in.

"It was all a coincidence. It's not possible," Hannah interrupted.

It was like we'd all been dying to get this off our chests and reveal the big secret.

Darbie ignored Hannah and told Frankie about the "Beware of the Law of Returns" note and the bad things that happened: Hannah being stung by bees, me having to carry Charlotte's books, her falls, and Mrs. Silvers going to the hospital.

"You sent some lady to the hospital? What did you do to her, knock her over?"

"Kelly brought her some juice," she said.

He stopped mid-sip. "Whoa. Stop right there. Brought her some *juice*? That sounds familiar."

"Well . . ." Darbie hesitated.

"Oh, man," he said with a big shake of his head. He took a hard sip of his thick drink. "I'm gonna be flippin' mad if you guys got me cursed."

"You're not *cursed*," Hannah said. She blew her bangs out of her face with gale force, clearly annoyed with Darbie and me.

Darbie said, "Since the three of us couldn't agree whether there was really something special about these recipes, we thought we would do an experiment."

"That sounds logical. Coach Richards would be very proud of you for testing your hypothesis." He slurped up the last droplets in his glass. "And how did you plan on doing that?"

Darbie looked to us for approval, but I didn't know what she should say. I didn't think he was gonna like the idea of us giving him a love potion. Not to mention that Hannah would die of embarrassment. I could already see her face flushing a shade of Bubblegum Swirley.

"By creating a love potion," Darbie said.

I saw the heat of anger fume out of Hannah's ears. In an effort to contradict Darbie, she said, "There are no potions. There is no curse. It's like a superstition or a self-fulfilling prophecy—if someone *thinks* that a black cat crossing his path will bring him bad luck, then it will."

Frankie said, "I don't believe in this stuff either."

I took a sip of my drink to wash the lump of embarrassment out of my throat. "These things can't *all* be coincidences. That would be too much of a coincidence."

Frankie stared at the bottom of his glass. "I don't believe it."

There was no way to avoid it. I had to ask him. "Then why did you fall in love with me after you drank the love potion?"

Hannah's straw fell out of her open mouth. This could be her final moment before she died of humiliation.

The tops of Frankie's ears reddened. "You potioned me?" Then he got louder. "I was right, you guys are crazy!" He went to take a swallow of his drink and realized that it was gone. "Sam!" he called. "Can I have another?"

It felt like a two Swirley sort of day. "Me too." I said. Then I checked out the other two empty glasses. "Actually, can you make everyone a refill?"

I couldn't tell if Frankie was shocked or angry. He didn't speak for a minute. But when he did, he asked the next logical question. "And *who* exactly was I supposed to fall in love *with*?"

I saw Darbie ready to open her mouth. I couldn't do this to Hannah. I had to jump in before Darbie told him. "You came into Home Ec saying all those nice things to me," I said.

"He did?" Hannah asked, confused.

"Whoa, whoa, whoa, whoooooa! Kell, you're a cool girl and all, but potion or no potion, I totally did *not* fall in love with you."

"You didn't?" I asked.

He combed both of his hands through his hair the way my father does when I drive him crazy. "I was being nice to you because . . . because. I didn't want to be in Home Ec. I don't want to cook. And if I don't keep my grades up, including flippin' Home Ec, I have to quit working. I thought you would do the assignments for me."

There was an uncomfortable silence. He wasn't in love with me? Maybe he *was* in love with me, only he didn't realize it.

I said, "Maybe you just think you aren't in love with me because of the Moon Honey."

"What's that?" he asked.

"The antidote to the Love Bug Juice," Darbie said.

He looked at me with confusion and anger in his eyes. "An antidote—"

I said, "Yeah. I sort of gave you one just now in your Swirley."

He nodded and looked at his cardboard box. "And the cannoli?"

Darbie said, "That was a way to get you down here so we could prove to Hannah that the juice worked by showing her you had fallen in love with Kelly. Good plan, huh?" She smiled.

Frankie didn't. "Great plan." He was furious.

Hannah made squinty little eyes at me and Darbie. "Well, it looks like your big experiment was a flop, which proves my theory. There are no potions." I'm sure she was angry with me for not telling her about Frankie falling for me, but she should have just been glad that we got through the entire rendezvous without him knowing that Hannah was actually the target for his affection.

Frankie asked Hannah, "What's with the pink glob on your face?"

She touched her cheek self-consciously, then looked at the cream on her fingertips. Her face turned the same color as the lotion that she wiped off with a paper napkin. "I can't believe you guys didn't remind me that was there," she said to us quietly, so that it didn't appear to Frankie that she was furious.

Sam brought four giant glasses full of Swirley goodness to the table.

There were no more brain freezes, and no more talking with Frankie—or with each other.

But I didn't buy that the experiment had failed. Quite the opposite, actually. Frankie could've just asked me to help him with Home Ec. I would've said yes. He had been into me, and the Moon Honey had snapped him out of it.

21

A Good Deed

Question: *If there was a smell, any smell, that I could choose to not smell for a year, what would it be?*

Answer: *Chili.*

After the meeting at Sam's, I came home to several pots simmering on the stove. I had to do two things: get antidotes to Mrs. Silvers and Charlotte Barney to undo hexes, and think of some really good things I could do to end my bad luck. I looked around the house, but your average chore wouldn't cut it. I needed something unexpected. Something out of the ordinary. Something I really didn't want to do.

The chili looked warm and bubbly. . . . The kind of thing that would be nice for an old woman on a cool afternoon.

I filled a plastic container with some chili, but before

securing the lid, I plunked in a cube of Moon Honey. It dissolved instantly.

Armed with the warm container and my pooper-scooper, I headed across the street.

I knocked on Mrs. Silvers's door.

Joanne answered. I gave her the chili, explaining that it was for Mrs. Silvers because we were all really hoping she'd be feeling better very soon, and that it was for our entry in the annual contest, which was in two days.

"What a lovely surprise," said Joanne. "Maybe Mom and I will stop by the contest. She might want to get out for a bit."

After I scooped the poop out of Mrs. Silvers's yard— *without being asked*—I also checked the yards of six other nearby houses and scooped anything suspicious.

Out of the corner of my eye I saw the curtain move in the downstairs window of Mrs. Silvers's house.

In one outing across the street, I'd delivered the anti-dote *and* done my good deed.

And that is, as my dad would say, how you kill two birds with one stone.

22

Isla de Cedros

Rosey chased after the leaves blowing around our backyard. Charlotte's lawn was covered with a thick blanket of unraked leaves. We just had to win the contest or I'd be raking for days. I felt really good about the concoction Mom and I had come up with this year. We actually had a chance of winning. But if we didn't . . . I looked at Charlotte's yard again.

I thought about the 1953 *World Book Encyclopedia* peeking out from under my bed, and I asked myself something that Darbie had asked days ago:

Question: If the recipe book made someone lose their voice,
go to the hospital, get foot blisters, and fall in love, why can't it
ensure that the Quinns take home the chili pepper necklace?

Answer: Actually, it could! But at the cost of a return.

I studied the thick, worn stationery pages, looking for something that might work for Mr. Douglass' taste buds.

At the bottom of one of the pages was a very simple recipe. It didn't have a title, but I could tell by looking at it that it was homemade vanilla ice cream. Next to the instructions was a note: "If made with vanilla beans from the western shore of the *Isla de Cedros*, enhances *la narize* and *la boca—rs*. Google confirmed that *narize* was "nose" and *boca* was "mouth." I also Googled *rs*, but no English translation came up. I wondered if *ip* and *rs* were a special code. I played with the letters, but I couldn't spell anything: spir, risp . . . nothing.

I did a search on *Isla de Cedros*. It's a Mexican island in the Pacific Ocean that was discovered by the Spanish and became a rich farming community.

I investigated our vanilla supply. We had vanilla extract, but the bottle didn't say anything about where it was grown. Normally, I would've used it anyway, but the note in the Book specifically said "if" made with vanilla beans from the western shore of the *Isla de Cedros*, the vanilla ice cream would enhance smell and taste. So the detail seemed pretty important.

I knew where I'd be able to get the Mexican vanilla beans, but I didn't want to go there.

At least not alone.

There was no sign of Charlotte around the neighborhood Saturday morning. I tried to resist, but I was too curious. I had to know if my nice scooping might've changed my luck. I went to her door.

"Hello Kelly," Mrs. Barney said.

"Is Charlotte here?"

"No, I'm sorry dear. She and her dad already left for tryouts. Did you need a ride?"

"No, thanks. I'm all set."

"Well, I'll tell her you stopped by, but you'll probably see her before I do. By the way, it's been so nice of you to help Charlotte with her books, but I think Mr. Barney is going to drive her to school for the next few days, so she won't need you anymore."

"Sure." I said. Okay, now I was truly excited.

"Better get going or you'll be late for soccer."

I ran home and got into the minivan, and we picked up Darbie.

"Guess what?" I whispered so Mom couldn't hear.

"Okay. I'll guess. What?" Darbie asked.

"I scooped the poop for the whole block last night, and now Charlotte is going to get rides to school from her dad. I don't have to carry her books!"

"Great," she said flatly.

The car stopped at a red light, right next to a Rusamano Landscaping truck. Tony looked out the window and gave us a little wave. Frankie looked out the other window.

"I think it's safe to say he's not in love with me anymore."

"Guess not." Darbie yawned.

"What's up with you?"

"I was up late last night and I'm very tired. Wake me up when we get to school."

Soccer tryouts buzzed with whispers. Today was the day we found out who made the cut. I saw Hannah. It looked like her bee stings had healed. She was with Charlotte.

Hannah. Sat. With. Charlotte.

I heard Hannah telling her, "You'll definitely make the team."

Stretching my neck, I spied in Hannah's direction. She asked Charlotte, "How are your blistery feet? I hope they'll be good enough to play in the game tomorrow."

Charlotte said, "Me too." She looked at me suspiciously.

I tapped Hannah's arm lightly, and out of the corner of my mouth I whispered, "Does the Wicked One have you under a trance?" I was only half joking.

Hannah took my elbow and moved a few steps away, out of earshot from Charlotte. "Kelly, I've wanted to tell you something for a while. You need to let go of your obsession with Charlotte. You can't get jealous every time I talk to her."

"Are you kidding me?" I asked. "Are you flippin' kidding me? I'm not jealous. I'm trying to protect you."

"Get serious."

"I am," I said. "Do you remember third grade?"

Hannah blew her bangs way high. "Yes, I've heard it all a hundred times. She told you about your surprise birthday party, so it wasn't a surprise anymore. It was horrible, terrible, very mean. But you still had an awesome party, and it was *years ago*. GET OVER IT!"

I huffed and maneuvered myself away from an angry Hannah, and closer to Darbie, who asked, "What's going on?"

"I think Hannah's on her way to Crazytown. And I'm pretty sure she's mad at me."

Darbie asked, "Can you blame her?"

What the heck is happening here?

"What?" I asked defensively.

"She kind of has a right to be mad at you for not telling her Frankie was in love with you, tricking him into coming to Sam's, and not telling her she looked like a circus sideshow."

"Maybe," I said. "But you didn't tell her either."

"I have an excuse. I don't notice crap like that. It's the way I am," Darbie said. "But she expects more from you."

"Great, so everything is all my fault," I ranted.

"OMG, will you chill, drama-monster?"

"I'm chilled—until Hannah gets attacked by something flying or crawling or buzzing," I said.

Coach gathered us up. "Okay. This is the last practice before the big game. I'm going to do something I've never done before. I'm not going to tell you who made the team today."

We peppered him with questions. "Why not?" "How come?" "What?"

"Simmer down, simmer down. I want to see everyone in a game situation. So, tomorrow all of you will play in the St. Mary's Spiders game. Wear a solid white shirt. Whoever makes the team will get an official Alfred Nobel uniform after the game, so you'll have it for the chili contest." He started stretching his legs.

We stretched too, like we were playing an assumed game of Simon Says. That's when I noticed something. In the distance I saw Tony Rusamano ride his bike past the field. He hopped off and watched us stretch for a few minutes.

"You know what we're going to do, right?" Coach yelled enthusiastically.

"Run," the girls answered—with a lot less excitement than Coach Richards.

"That's right! Let's GOOOO."

We ran laps around the field, Hannah in the lead.

"What are you doing later?" I asked Darbie.

"Something nice." She gritted her teeth. "My stinking good deed. Thanks to Señora Goody-Two-Shoes, I'm going to finish the chores I started last night. Can you believe it? I'm washing lawn furniture and putting it in the basement. It sucks."

"Maybe it does." I watched Darbie run for a bit. "But have you noticed that you're not tripping anymore?"

"Yeah. But I'm still not happy about the chores. I don't like chores. I hate chores. I do anything I can to avoid them. Sometimes, I even do homework just so that I don't have to take out the trash. It's the kind of person I am. I'm a non-chore-doer." Darbie was snippy in a way that was totally unlike her. "And if it wasn't for that book, I wouldn't be in this crappy-chore stinkfest."

"Oh. Sorry about that," I said, as nonclumsy Darbie ran ahead without me.

What's happening here? Am I seriously fighting with my two best friends?

Coach had half of us run up and down the bleachers. From the top I had a great view of the Alfred Nobel campus and the whole soccer field. Darbie took some shots on goal, which were really good—high and to the corner. On the other side of the field, Hannah spoke to Charlotte. It made my belly simmer like a pot of chili left on a hot stove. Charlotte laughed. But Hannah? Not so much. On the street side of the field, I saw Tony ride by again.

On my next climb to the top of the bleachers, I noticed that Charlotte wasn't laughing anymore. Hannah's hands were propped on her hips, and she leaned forward as she talked, her mouth flapping frantically.

I ran back up the bleachers again. No Tony, and Darbie scored. Hannah dribbled the ball away from Charlotte. Charlotte looked like she called after Hannah. Hannah didn't respond. I wondered if those two had a spat.

I ran down and toward the field, passing Darbie on her way to do the bleacher routine. I asked her, "Hey, after practice, do you think you could—"

"No," she said. "After practice I have to go straight home and finish my work."

"Oh." I officially had no one to go with me to La Cocina—I was on my own.

The store was quiet, with no customers. There were never any customers. But I was not alone—I was surrounded by glassy-eyed dead animals. Somehow, their presence wasn't comforting.

Since I knew how the spices were organized, I went to

the shelf that contained items starting with the letter *V.*
It was next to the framed beach photo I had seen before.
Only this time I read the inscription on the frame's golden
plaque: ISLA DE CEDROS.

A noise behind me startled me. "Excuse me, *chica.* I
didn't mean to frighten you."

Lurker!

I should've been used to her scaring the crap out of me
by now, but I wasn't. Señora Perez could tell.

She looked at the photo with sadness in her face. "It's
beautiful, *no?*"

I nodded.

"It is a very special place with a special story."

My voice hadn't found its way back to my *boca* yet.

"Would you like to hear it?" she asked.

I nodded again.

"In the old days, *Isla de Cedros* was attacked by pirates.
The peaceful towns were small and defenseless. To protect
themselves, the village's spiritual guide, we call him the
shaman, enchanted the farmers' spices. The farmers used
these spices to protect their families. Other herbs were
packed into their treasures.

"The next time the pirates looted the villages and sailed
away with the villagers' riches, a storm followed them. It
dragged the pirates and the treasures far out to sea, where
the ships and their contents sank."

"Were the treasures ever found?" I asked.

"No. The Cedronians believed their island was safer with their jewels and coins at the bottom of the ocean, because without any treasures, the pirates would leave them alone."

"But then the islanders wouldn't have any treasure," I said.

"But they did. They had family and friends and their beautiful *Isla de Cedros. That* was their treasure. And, of course, they still had their special spices," Señora Perez said.

I said, "That's exactly what I need."

"Really?"

"Yes. Vanilla bean from *Isla de Cedros.* Do you have any?"

She paused and looked at me strangely. "*Si*, I have vanilla bean from *Isla de Cedros.*" Instead of taking something from the *V* shelf, she reached for a canister. She took out a little bag, small enough to be a pillowcase for an ant. She dipped a spoon into the canister to retrieve a scoop of beans, which she poured into the pillowcase. Then she cut off several inches of twine and tied the pillowcase closed. "These beans will enhance the senses of smell and taste," she said.

"Yes, that's what I was hoping." I held out my hand casually, hoping she'd give me the beans without asking more questions.

She dropped the sack into my hand. I reached into my pocket for money, but she waved me off.

"*Gracias*," I said.

"And don't forget," she said. "*Quien siembra vient—*"

"I know, I know. The Law of Returns."

She smiled. "How did doing good deeds work to balance the bad luck?"

"I think mine worked. Darbie's still at it. And she's not happy about it."

"If it's easy, it won't affect the forces of nature," she said. "And Hannah?"

"She's not talking to me much today."

"Sometimes you need to make sacrifices for a special friend," she said. "That is true kindness."

"I guess," I said, and walked toward the door. But I wasn't sure what she meant.

I paused before leaving. "Señora Perez, do you believe in magic?"

"Of course. What would the world be like without magic? I do not think I want to know."

"What about magic books?" I asked.

"I believe many things are magical—stars, knowledge, poetry, love, and friendship. But books? *No*, they are just paper, ink, and words. Not magical."

I nodded and slowly walked to the door. When I turned my head to say *adios*, she was gone.

23
Condensed Soup

I hated Charlotte. I'd never been shy about that fact. But I wanted to make a sacrifice for my friend Hannah. I knew she really wanted to win our soccer game, and she wanted Charlotte to make the team. This was more likely to happen if Charlotte played so that Coach could see how good she was. So, I needed to undo those blistered feet.

I set my Cedronian vanilla beans aside in exchange for the Moon Honey, which I took with me. Before knocking on Charlotte's back door, I peeked through the window to get the lay of the land.

I had been in the Barneys' kitchen a million times to feed

their cat while they were away. It looked like it could be on the cover of a designer magazine. The wallpaper was yellow with cheerful little teapots. The floor was shiny hardwood, the appliances brushed stainless steel, and there was a bouquet of fresh flowers on the center of the kitchen table.

This was a kitchen made to *look* like someone cooks in it. Actually, it saw only takeout Chinese, pizza boxes, plastic to-go containers, and precooked frozen dinners. What a bummer that all of this fabulous cooking space went to waste.

I saw two empty cans of condensed soup on the counter, their contents in a silver pot. A wooden spoon stuck straight up in the soup, which was still in the shape of cans.

The table was set with three bowls and three glasses— two of them wine glasses, one a regular drinking glass.

I resisted the urge to go home, whip up a pot of my awesome homemade chicken-and-rice soup with fresh parsley and long-grained wild rice, bring it over, and swap out the pots, so that the Barneys could have a decent dinner. But I figured that could be something nice I could do the next time I needed good luck.

I knocked on the back door and after a minute Charlotte came.

"What do *you* want?"

I didn't pretend that I suddenly liked her. "Can I borrow your Spanish notes? I forgot mine in my locker."

"Sure, for five dollars."

"You've gotta be kidding me."

She folded her arms across her chest. "Nope."

"Fine."

She held out her hand.

"I don't have it on me. I'll give it to you tomorrow."

She guffawed. "I know where you live. If I don't get it tomorrow, I'll start charging you interest."

"Fine. Look, can I just borrow your notes?"

"Wait here," she said, as if I'd track mud all over the white carpets.

When she was gone, I approached the table, took a honey drop, and wiped it around and around the inside of the bowl near the regular drinking glass. It took a lot of swirls to coat the inside of the bowl. I was still swirling when I heard footsteps coming toward the kitchen. They were coming fast. I took the remaining stub of honey drop and put it in my pocket.

I scrambled back to where I had been before Charlotte left, but she saw me moving.

"What were you just doing?" she asked, like she'd caught me with my hand in the cookie jar.

"Nothing. Well, actually, you caught me. I was dancing. You know how you get a song in your head that you can't get out?" That seemed to satisfy her.

"Here." She tossed me the notes like they were a hot tamale.

"Thanks," I said.

"Don't thank me. It's a business deal. I'll expect my money tomorrow."

"Fine."

I went home, but before I reached the door, something totally annoying happened. I stepped in dog poop.

I could've interpreted this in many ways, but I thought it was probably a reminder from the Law of Returns that good deeds take some time and they can't be easy. So I went to Mrs. Silvers's yard, scraping my shoe on the sidewalk, the street, and the grass. For the second night, I scooped without being asked, another pleasant surprise for the Silvers residence.

I was proud of myself for successfully doling out another antidote. I wanted to do a little happy dance, but I didn't feel happy enough. The dance wasn't the same without the girls there. I couldn't be happy enough to dance when I knew they were mad at me. The reasons they were mad at me were because of the Secret Recipe Book—a book that, according to Señora Perez, couldn't be magic.

My BFF trio felt like it was crumbling like a stale corn muffin, all because of the Book.

Question: *Is the Book worth my BFFs being mad at me?*

That night I went to bed, with Rosey's cold nose on my ankle, and with no answer.

24

ANtS vs. Spiders

"Every stupid piece of stupid lawn furniture has been cleaned and is packed away. I'm ready for a non-clumsy day, and if I don't get it, I might have to pop that Señora in the nose," Darbie said to me. "So let's get this game on."

"Does that mean you're not mad at me anymore?" I asked.

"Mad? That wasn't mad. That was tired and cranky. I get that way. You should know the difference by now, Kelly Q."

"I'm not sure I've ever seen you *that* cranky."

"This is seventh grade. It's a whole new world." Darbie

patted me on the back. "I'll try to go easier on you next time."

Coach Richards looked official in his ANtS Athletics shirt and shorts. And even in unofficial solid white shirts, we looked sort of like a team ourselves.

After a lap and stretch he said, "Girls, bring yourselves in here." On our way to huddle up, I overheard him ask Charlotte if her feet felt up to playing.

"You bet, Coach. I'm good to go," she said.

Ta-da! Go Moon Honey! Go Moon Honey!

I could tell that Hannah heard Charlotte. I expected her to at least crack a smile, but her face remained flat.

Why?

The game flew by. Darbie played goalie, while Hannah and Charlotte were on offense. I was on the bench. In between plays I heard Mr. Douglass giving the play-by-play over the loudspeaker. Thankfully it was a low-tech, low-budget audio system, so the Spiders and their parents couldn't hear him.

Hannah dominated the offense immediately. She scored, thanks to an assist from Charlotte.

I might have even forgotten that Charlotte is evil by the way she was playing. Hannah's expression wasn't flat anymore. She was psyched by her goal. Then, within a few minutes, she set up Charlotte to score.

"The ANtS are ahead two to zero," Mr. Douglass announced.

I went in just in time for the Spiders to get a breakaway.

"The Spiders score!" Mr. Douglass yelled. "What a bummer. Don't worry, Darbie. Even Martha Stewart with a wok wouldn't have been able to block that shot."

We held them off until the fourth quarter, when the Spiders scored again, tying up the game.

Hannah jogged off the field and talked to Coach Richards. Then Coach put Hannah in as goalie, and Darbie and me on offense. It was all up to us.

Mr. Douglass described the action. "O'Brien runs the ball down the center and passes it. Oh, the Spiders get the ball. Wait, Kelly Quinn gets it back. Look at that fancy footwork. She's dribbling straight toward that Spider! Now what? Quinn passes *backward* to O'Brien. Quinn gives O'Brien the perfect shot—and the ANtS score!"

Darbie jumped up and down and did an overly energetic happy dance that hip-checked Charlotte, who had come over to give her a high five.

The referee blew the whistle. The crowd exploded with applause. I think I heard Tony Rusamano's voice among the cheers.

The game ended with an ANtS victory.

Darbie ran toward me with a recognizable look in her eye. I could tell she was going to try to chest-bump me. I braced myself.

"Ouch!" Mr. Douglass said over the loudspeaker.

"Quinn is on the ground, decked by her teammate."

"Oops, sorry, Kell," Darbie said, offering her hand to help me up.

Hannah ran over and gave us a big hug. Our victory seemed to have made her forget that she was mad at me.

Mr. Douglass concluded with an important invitation. "Please join us here later for the Annual Alfred Nobel Chili Cook-Off, which will be judged by YOURS TRULY!"

We gathered around Coach Richards. "Great game, girls! I'm very proud of you." He patted a lot of backs. "Get some water and let's talk." The thirsty team chugged from their water bottles. "You all did a great job today," Coach said. "You should be proud of yourselves. It's time to announce who made the team."

Everyone stopped drinking.

"I've decided I'm going to take everyone this year. You all made it!"

"YAY!" There was a round of hugs.

We did a dance and pumped our arms. Darbie took a few steps back and came at me for a chest bump, which went terribly wrong because she tripped and ended up on the ground.

"Maybe it's time to give up the chest bumps," I said.

Darbie agreed.

Hannah pulled her off the ground.

Coach said, "Calm down, calm down." We did. "Do you see that lady over there?" he asked. "That's Erin, the department assistant. If you're very nice to her, and tell her what a great coach I am, she'll give you your uniforms."

"Let's go before all the good numbers are taken," I said to the girls.

Darbie ran full speed toward Erin. I felt badly for that woman, as the chances of her being laid out in the next few minutes were pretty high. "O'Brien!" Coach yelled. She stopped and looked at him. "Chill," he said. Darbie slowed to a fast walk.

"Can I have number six? Or number twelve?" she asked.

Before going home, I gave Charlotte the five dollars I owed her. She tried to make a big deal about it, which I didn't want to hear, so I just walked away. As I did, I thought I saw Tony Rusamano riding away on his bike.

25

The Annual Chili Cook-Off . . . Finally

We crossed the schoolyard toward the Chili Cook-Off. I felt as though my luck was changing, and I owed it all to that fabulous antidote called Moon Honey.

It had been a great day for the ANtS soccer team. Everyone played well, including Darbie. I had to give myself a big ol' pat on the back for successfully getting the antidote to Charlotte so that she was able to play. We might have lost the game if it weren't for her big assist.

"So, your feet are better?" I asked her.

"Oh yeah. Once I stopped wearing those new cleats, they were fine."

I nodded, even though I knew it really had nothing to do with the cleats.

"But you can still carry my books if you want," she added in typical Charlotte style.

I noticed Hannah shoot a harsh look in her direction.

"Fat chance," Darbie said, and pulled us toward the mariachi band playing the "Macarena." "Do you think she could have gotten rid of her blisters that fast by changing her shoes?" Darbie asked.

Hannah said, "I think it depends on how bad they were in the first place. But I think if you keep them clean, or go to the doctor, they can get better very quickly."

None of us said what Hannah's comment could mean, but I read her mind. She thought the blisters had nothing to do with the Secret Recipe Book and that their cure had nothing to do with the Moon Honey.

"Ouch!" *Smack.* "Gotcha," Hannah said to the mosquito on her arm. Actually, she had several bites on her arm.

"Haven't you done anything nice yet?" I asked.

Hannah said, "It's just a mosquito. Don't make it something it isn't."

I dropped the topic and we entered the school parking lot, which was full of colorful chili pepper lights and decorations. Tables were set up on either side of an Astroturf pathway. Tiki torches and orange paper lanterns marked the pathway. The smell of chili clouded the air.

The contestants had decorated their own tables. Most people used bright cloth paper lanterns and signage identifying who they were. Mom was standing by her table handing out samples of her chili in little Styrofoam bowls along with brightly colored napkins.

People parked cars up and down the street to get a taste of the action. But the only opinion that really mattered was Mr. Douglass'. It looked like he was starting the judging with Mrs. R.

A hush fell over the crowd as he prepared himself to sample the four-time champion's chili. All eyes were glued on the Home Ec teacher as he gave a bizarre performance. He pulled a purple bandana out of his back pocket and blindfolded himself. He moved his longish, slender nose over the steam lifting from his bowl. He registered no facial expression as he dipped only the tip of his plastic spoon into the chili and delivered it to his pursed lips. He savored the stew for a moment before chewing with a look of deep concentration. After swallowing, he slid his tongue around the inside of his mouth, visibly exploring his cheeks and teeth without so much as a hint whether he liked it or not.

The ritual was painfully slow and detailed, so I scanned the crowd. I was surprised at who I saw walking from a handicapped parking space: Mrs. Silvers with a walker and her daughter helping her to navigate the parking lot. She approached the tables.

I tapped Darbie on the shoulder. "Look," I said.

"That Moon Honey must be some powerful stuff to get her up and around," she said.

Hannah turned to see what we were staring at. "What's on her face?" she asked.

"I think it's a smile," I said.

"Scary," Darbie added.

Mrs. Silvers and her daughter walked toward us. "Hello, girls." Joanne eyed our uniforms. "Looks like you made the team." She waved to someone in the crowd of Mr. Douglass watchers.

"Did you win?" Mrs. Silvers asked. Her voice was husky and there was something strange about it . . . something that I couldn't put my finger on.

"Yep," Hannah offered.

"Thanks for the sneak preview of your chili," Mrs. Silvers said. That might've been the most I'd ever heard her say without yelling. *That's* what was different about her voice. She wasn't yelling. "It was so good, I wanted to come get some more," she continued.

"I'm glad you liked it," I said.

Darbie and Hannah seemed mesmerized by this woman who had invaded Mrs. Silvers's body. "When did they let you out of the hospital?" Darbie asked as though

Mrs. Silvers had been let out of prison. Before she had a chance to answer, Darbie added, "And what were you in for?" Then, under her breath, "A personality transplant?"

No one else heard, but I nudged her to shut up.

"Oh, I was just in for one night," Mrs. Silvers replied. "Partial knee replacement." She lifted up the bottom of her housedress, which solved an old mystery—she did, in fact, have feet. *Who knew?* She also revealed a rather gruesome zipper scar that hadn't fully healed on her knee. "Check that out."

"Holy stromboli," Darbie said. "That's a beaut." Hannah and I looked away from the bruised and swollen joint.

Mrs. Silvers laughed. *The woman laughed.*

"Does it hurt?" Hannah asked.

"Sure, a bit. But I'm taking pain medicine, so it's not too bad. And it's going to be much better than it was before. Oh, it always hurt so badly before."

Back in the crowd Mr. Douglass finished his work at the Rusamano table. He politely thanked Mrs. R. and moved along to the next table, writing in his judge's notebook on his way. Then I saw Mrs. Eagle emerge from the crowd holding a little shopping bag by the handle. She handed the bag to Joanne. "Herrre you go. Therrre's a containerrr frrrom each table."

"Thank you, Mrs. Eagle," Joanne said. Mrs. Eagle simply nodded and returned to the group of women staring at Mr.

Douglass' every move. "She was the librarian when I went to school here."

"Lovely woman," Mrs. Silvers added.

Lovely? Not a word I would've used to describe Mrs. Eagle.

"Oh, wait a minute," Mrs. Silvers said. "I almost forgot. I saw something I thought you might be interested in, Kelly." She balanced herself carefully on her walker before pushing one hand into her muumuu's pocket. She took out an ad from a folded magazine. "Here."

I unfolded it and read. Hannah and Darbie read over my shoulder. "Felice Foudini is hosting a recipe challenge. You submit your recipe and the one she likes best, wins. The prize is money and a visit from Felice herself!" I recapped. "This is awesome. Thank you."

"You're welcome," Mrs. Silvers said. "I heard you were an aspiring chef, so I thought you would be interested."

I said, "I love Felice Foudini."

"Well, good luck," Mrs. Silvers said.

Then Joanne said, "It was nice seeing you, but we're going to head back home and elevate Mom's leg again. We just wanted to get out for a moment of fresh air."

We said our good-byes and watched Joanne help the woman claiming to be Mrs. Silvers get back into the car.

As we watched her leave, I said, "I think we all just made a personal visit to Crazytown."

Darbie added, "Serious twilight zone. I think I have goose bumps. I mean, who the heck *was* that? Did you hear that laugh?"

"Those must have been some powerful moonbeams," I said.

Hannah giggled a bit. "Moonbeams, schmoonbeams. Do I need to point out to you that you *didn't* send her to the hospital? That kind of operation is planned way ahead of time."

Hannah had a point. Maybe I hadn't sent her to the hospital—but then I hadn't reversed anything either. Maybe I'd just given an old lady some chili with a dab of honey.

26

And the Winner Is . . .

Darbie said, "I'm gonna get me some of Mrs. R.'s chili before it's all gone. I'm so hungry my ribs are showing."

"Me too," Hannah said.

We wiggled our way to the front of the Rusamano's table.

"Hey, Mrs. R.," Darbie said. "How are you?"

"Hello, girls." She gave us each a kiss on the cheek. "Congratulations, Frankie told me about the big game."

"Where is Frankie?" Hannah asked. Mrs. R.'s lip curled up a bit as she scraped three bowls of chili out of the bottom of the pot.

"Mr. R. set up a warmer in the back of one of the land-scaping trucks," she said. "Frankie and Tony went to get me some more pots. The chili's going fast. I hope I don't run out."

Not a second later we heard Frankie. "Excuse me, coming through." Behind him, also carrying a pot, was Tony. I noticed something on Tony's arms that I'd never noticed before: muscles. Behind Tony was Mr. R.

"*Scusi,* hot stuff. And I'm not talking 'bout the chili!" Mr. R. laughed loudly. He placed a huge silver pot where his wife pointed. She was prepared to feed a small country.

"Hi, girls," Frankie said. "So, whatcha think of the chili? Good, huh?" I guess he wasn't mad about being potioned anymore. Boys are like that—they can get over stuff faster than girls, who make a big deal out of everything.

Darbie said, "It's good."

While Darbie and Hannah chatted with the Rusamanos, I approached Mom. "Mom, where's the cooler I packed?"

"In the car." She didn't look at me. She was focused on the man walking toward her table. It was Mr. Douglass with a glass of water.

Quickly I got the cooler, which contained my lunch Thermos. Inside my lunch Thermos was a cup of the home-made ice cream with vanilla bean from *Isla de Cedros.* I put some ice cream into a Styrofoam bowl.

Mr. Douglass approached our table and put his hand on

my shoulder. "Hello, Kelly. And you must be Mrs. Quinn. You've raised a future chef in this girl. She's my brightest student."

"Don't I know it. She'd make Felice Foudini proud. You know Kelly was on her television show several years ago?"

"She was? Kelly, you didn't tell me that. I read her blog every day. I would love to meet her."

I said, "I don't really keep in touch with her."

Mr. Douglass said, "We should get Miss Foudini to come to Alfred Nobel to be a guest chef. Oh, and maybe next year we can be co-judges."

"Really?" I asked. "That would be amazing."

"What's that?" he asked, looking at my bowl of ice cream.

"Oh, nothing. It was just some ice cream. But it wasn't very good." I took the ice cream intended to enhance his taste buds right before he tried our chili and pitched it into the nearby trash can. I couldn't do it. He was so nice to me, and he thought I was a good cook.

Mom handed Mr. Douglass a bowl of her chili. "Now, what we've done this year is interesting. We've . . ."

Mr. Douglass ignored Mom as he fixated on getting himself into judge character. He set down the chili and blindfolded himself.

Mom watched Mr. Douglass inhale the steam rising from the bowl. His expression was unchanged. Mom wrung her hands. "Does he look like he likes it?" she whispered to me.

"I think he always looks like that," I whispered back.

Mr. Douglass finished his tasting ritual, took off the blindfold, and Mom invaded his personal space bubble. "So?" she asked.

"Thank you, Mrs. Quinn." He took her hand, bent at the waist, and kissed it. "*Enchanté.*" And then he walked away, writing in his notebook.

"Do you think he liked it?" asked my mom. "He kissed my hand. I don't think he kissed Lucia Rusamano's hand. He looked like he liked it, I think."

"I'm sure he liked it, Mom—and that Felice thing has to go a long way. He's a huge fan."

"Yeah. Sure. Of course he liked it." Mom walked away from the table still babbling to herself. "Why wouldn't he like it?"

Pat, pat went the microphone.

Darbie stood next to me. "I saw what you did with the ice cream. I just want to know why?"

Now Hannah was on the other side of me. "Because Mrs. Silvers just confirmed that there are no potions in the Book," she said.

"Actually," I said, "it just felt like cheating."

"TESTING, *un, deux, trois.*" Mr. Douglass stood at a podium decorated with chili pepper garden lights. "May I have everyone's attention, please? Thank you to all of this year's contestants and to all of you tasters. All of the dishes were wonderfully impressive. But there can only be one winner. And the winner of the Alfred Nobel Chili Cook-Off is . . ."

I held my breath and crossed my fingers.

". . . Lucia Rusamano!"

The crowd cheered.

My mom clapped, but I saw her body deflate and her shoulders hunch into her "bummed-out Mom" posture.

The next half hour passed with very little talking. Dad loaded a bunch of stuff into his car, including Buddy, who was snoozing, and they headed for home.

Hannah and Darbie got into Mom's minivan. The parking lot slowly emptied.

"Good night, Lucia," Mom said to Mrs. R. "Congratulations." She forced a smile.

"*Grazie*, Becky." She walked over and gave my mom a kiss on each cheek before climbing into the landscaping truck.

"Bye, guys," Frankie said. "See you tomorrow." He climbed into the back of the truck and wrapped his arms around empty pots to keep them secure.

I was trying to lift a box into the back of the minivan when Frankie's twin brother, Tony, appeared. He loaded the last of the bowls and spoons into the landscaping truck and walked over to me.

"Kelly, let me help you with that," he said. I thought that was the most I'd ever heard Tony say. "Sorry about the contest. I know you really wanted to win."

Of everyone who could have acknowledged my disappointment, it was Tony Rusamano. "Thanks, Tony," I said.

He lifted the heavy box and easily slid it into the back of the minivan. Then he reached over my head to pull down the back hatch, and his arm brushed mine. His hand lingered next to mine for an extra beat or two. It felt like the frozen feathery feet of three hundred centipedes danced up my arms. When he moved his hand, he raised it to my cheek and I felt a—

"OOoch," I said in response to the shock.

"Sorry about that, you had a fuzzy thing on your face." His eyes were glued on me. A cool autumn breeze blew his bangs out of his face. I'd never really seen his eyes. They were hazel with flecks of gold and framed by incredibly long, dark eyelashes.

And then it happened: He leaned closer, right next to my ear. I smelled the fabric softener on his flannel shirt. "I'll see you tomorrow, Kelly," he said. I felt his warm breath on my neck.

Tony Rusamano brushed his hair aside. Then he winked and smiled at me.

I repeat: Tony Rusamano *blatantly* winked and smiled right at *me*, Kelly Quinn.

27
More Bug Juice

"Well, girls, you win some and you lose some," Mom said to us in the minivan.

"Keep your chin up, Mrs. Q.," Darbie said. "There's always next year."

Ordinarily I would've been furious about having to rake Charlotte's yard wearing I-can't-imagine-what. But right then, every section of my brain was preoccupied—no, obsessed—with two things: a wink and a smile.

We pulled into Sam's. "Thanks, Mom. I'll walk home." I hopped out of the van after the girls.

"Wait." Mom pulled me back. "I really liked doing this

contest with you," she said. Her eyes welled up.

Oh, holy guacamole. Here it was, a burst of maternal emotion.

"It was just so nice spending extra time with you," she said.

"It was fun for me too," I said. Hannah and Darbie had already disappeared into Sam's. "Maybe we could talk about this tonight, Mom."

She wiped her eyes. "Yes. Sure, of course we can. You go have some fun with the girls and celebrate making the team and your big victory. Don't worry about the contest, it's not important."

"Okay, but Mom, it was really fun."

The chili contest had always been the most exciting thing in our lives for the month of September, but this year I had been so busy with the Book that I sort of blew it off.

Because of the Book.

"Congratulations! Looks like you all made the team," Sam said. "I got a new flavor in today—German chocolate. And it's on me, so you can celebrate the new ANtS girls' soccer team."

"And we won our first game!" Hannah said.

"Terrific. That calls for free whipped cream, too."

Smirking, I whispered, "And that's not all."

The girls looked at me, confused.

We took our bowls to a table. I couldn't get my grin to relax.

"What's up with you?" Hannah asked. "I thought you'd be furious about Mrs. Silvers not being potioned, and the Book not being real."

"And about having to rake Charlotte's yard," Darbie said.

"I'm not thrilled about the raking gig. And for the record, the next time you want to open your big *boca* and make a bet for me, check with me first. Whatdoyasay, Darb?"

Her head bobbed.

"And I'm still thinking about the Silvers thing. That's an anomaly, as you scientific types say about data that doesn't make sense. But you're *never* going to believe what happened to me when I was packing up the minivan." I paused to make sure I had their complete attention. "You see, Hannah, you're wrong about the Book."

I explained the arm brush, hand linger, shock, whisper, wink, and smile.

"Tony?" Hannah asked.

"Tony," I confirmed. "And I've seen him hanging around at our practices and maybe at the game."

"Lurking?" Darbie joked.

"Sort of, I guess, but not in a creepy way."

"OMG! He likes you!" Darbie said.

"Tony? No way," Hannah said. "Maybe a chunk of his bangs fell into his eyes, making it look like he winked."

Darbie asked, "Why wouldn't Tony have a crush on Kelly? Besides being probably the coolest and most-liked girl in seventh grade, she's also one of the prettiest."

Was she talking about *me*?

Hannah said, "Of course she is, but this is Tony Rusamano we're talking about. He doesn't know what the word 'girl' means."

Darbie took a big spoonful of the German chocolate ice cream.

"That's exactly my point," I said. "There's no way he likes me ordinarily, which is what makes this so major. Remember when we brought Frankie the Love Bug Juice?"

They nodded.

"Tony drank some too. Remember? Before his graceful display of armpit farts?"

"Oh yeah, he did," Darbie said. "He makes some impressive sounds with that pit."

Sam yelled over, "How do you like the German chocolate?"

Only Darbie had even tasted it. Hannah and I stopped chattering and dipped our spoons into our ice cream. "Mmmm," I said.

"Best chocolate I've ever had," Hannah said. "The Germans know what they're talking about."

"Good. Good. Good." Sam wiped the glass at the counter where he kept his postcard collection. I walked over to grab some napkins and caught a glimpse of the picture on one of the postcards. I had seen it before. It was the beach from Señora Perez's photo.

I sat back down and Darbie said, "It's really good, but chocolate is chocolate to me."

"No way," Hannah said. "All chocolate is not created equal."

"Wait," I said. I stared into the distance as my brain cranked at warp speed.

"Brain freeze?" Darbie asked.

"No." I looked at Hannah. "What did you just say?"

"I said that all chocolate is not created equal."

"That's IT!" I yelled, and slammed my fist onto the table. "Hannah, you're a GENIUS!"

"I am?" she asked.

"She is?" Darbie asked.

"You have solved the puzzle of the Book!"

"What did I say?" she asked.

"All chocolate *isn't* the same. Neither is vanilla bean, or ginseng, or mint," I said. "Mexican mint is different."

"So?"

"That's why the Fresh Citrus Squeeze didn't work for Mrs. Silvers. I used mint from my house, from the supermarket. The recipe in the Book called for Mexican mint. You were completely right about Mrs. Silvers's operation.

It was planned. It had nothing to do with me."

"I'm glad to see you've finally come to your senses," Hannah said. "This is what I've been trying to convince you of for days."

"I didn't cause any strife because I didn't use the right ingredients. In the Keep 'Em Quiet Cobbler, the Hexberry Pie, and the Love Bug Juice we used the right ingredients— *special* ingredients."

Hannah blew her bangs out of her face and asked, "And now is this when you're going to tell us how they're special?"

I ignored her sarcasm. "All the other ingredients were from La Cocina. They were from *Isla de Cedros*."

"*Isla de* what?" Darbie asked.

I walked over to the counter. I pointed to the postcard through the glass. "Sam, may I borrow this for a second?"

"Sure, Kelly. Just be sure to give it back. My friend Ida Perez sent it to me last time she visited her home. I really like that picture," he said.

"Her home?"

"Yes, she's from an island near Mexico called—"

"*Isla de Cedros*?" I finished his thought.

He asked, "How did you know that?"

"Lucky guess." I gently slid the postcard out from under the glass. I turned it over and read the back.

Dear Sam,

Gracias for looking after the store.
See you when I get back.

Ida Perez.

Her signature was big, wavy, and flowy. The *I* in "Ida" was huge, followed by a huge *P* in "Perez."

"What's that?" Hannah asked as I walked back over to her and Darbie.

I showed them the picture. "This is *Isla de Cedros*. It's a Mexican island in the Pacific Ocean. It used to get attacked by pirates until the farmers and the shaman worked together to grow spices with protective powers to guard their families and villages. They also grew spices to pack with their treasures. The next time the pirates attacked, their ships sank and they all drowned."

Darbie said, "Now, that's one heck of a hex."

"You ain't kidding," I said.

Hannah said, "And you think vetivert, rue, and ginseng were all from this island, and that they somehow found their way to our cooking club in the small, East Coast town of Wilmington, Delaware. Kind of unlikely, donchathink?"

"Not if someone in Wilmington is from *Isla de Cedros*," I said.

They didn't know who I was talking about.

"And if this someone wrote a Secret Recipe Book," I added.

They were still confused.

I took a napkin, snatched a pen off the counter, and doodled "IP."

Darbie asked, "It all comes back to *ip*?"

I said, "It's not *ip*. It's an *I* and a *P*. They're initials." I turned the postcard over and showed them the signature line. 'IP' is Ida Perez. Señora Perez is from *Isla de Cedros*. She knows that the herbs grown on the western coast of the island are special. She sells them at La Cocina. The spices we bought from her have special powers."

Darbie said, "It's the ingredients that make the recipes into potions."

I nodded. "Exactly."

Darbie said, "The *ip* in the Book is Ida Perez."

Hannah didn't nod, but she didn't blow her bangs out of her face either. "It's Señora Perez's book," she said.

I nodded again. "Right."

"We need to go see that Señora," Darbie said.

28
The Story of the Book

You'll need:
3 BFFs
1 secretive Señora
1 island off the coast of Mexico
1 bunch of pirates
1 shaman

Directions:
Take it behind a curtain of beads, smoosh it all together inside a
mesh tea ball, and dunk it in mugs of steaming hot water.

It didn't take long for us to walk to La Cocina. Señora
Perez held open the string of beads. "Come back for
tea, *chicas*." Somehow she knew we were not there
to shop.

We followed her to the world behind the sheet of beads.
The room didn't look anything like I'd imagined. I had
expected heavy burgundy curtains, crystal balls, Victorian

chairs with high backs, and other mysterious fortune-teller stuff.

Instead, the floor was linoleum, lifted up and torn in several spots. There was one piece of furniture—an old metal kitchen table with matching folding chairs. There was a small counter space with a hot plate, some silver canisters, and a vase filled with utensils. On the wall, a mesh metal tea ball hung from a hook. A small shelf above the counter held a few cracked tea cups, chipped plates, mismatched bowls, and a kettle. There was no crystal ball to be found . . . not even a honeydew melon.

Señora Perez motioned for us to sit and filled the kettle with water from an oversize utility sink. She set the kettle on the hot plate and sat herself in the fourth chair. I looked at her closely—the pineapple bun on top of her head, the multiple scarves around her neck, her pointy nose that resembled a bird's beak. She didn't frighten me anymore. "You have questions," she began.

"*Si,*" I said.

"I wondered when you would come in with them."

Darbie leaned forward, her elbows and forearms on the table as though she was taking charge of the conversation. "We think we found something that belongs to you." Darbie said, like she was a TV detective mounting an investigation.

"My book," Señora Perez said.

Darbie seemed too surprised by this admission to continue her line of questioning. So, Hannah picked it up. "You know about the Book?"

"*Sí*. It's mine."

"Why didn't you say something?" Darbie asked.

"I was not certain until just now, but I had my suspicions the first day you came in."

"What did you suspect?" I asked in a tone more polite than Darbie's.

"I thought you were up to something, but I did not know what."

Darbie jumped in. "What made you think we were up to something? At that point we were totally normal customers."

"The ingredients you chose weren't the ones my normal customers buy," Señora Perez answered evenly, implying that she did in fact have customers, and that she thought they were normal. "But I sell them to you, and I tell you: *Quien siembra vientos recoge temtestades*, in case you are up to what I thought you were up to."

Darbie looked puzzled and paused, as if she was waiting for Señora Perez to continue her confession.

Señora Perez filled the quiet. "Then Kelly came in with a boy and bought shade-grown ginseng. Still, I wasn't sure you had the Book. Anyone can buy shade-grown ginseng, but no one ever does. The bottle for regular ginseng is right in the front and it is much prettier. People buy that one all the time. It's one of my most popular items. Everyone uses ginseng to make homemade love potions." She turned to look at me. "But you knew about the shade-grown ginseng. So I warned you again. But did you listen?"

She pointed to Darbie's legs. "You grow more bruises every day. I see," she said, pointing to her eyes. "I see your bee stings, too," she added, looking at Hannah. "And I know what Kelly has to do for the girl she does not like."

Through gritted teeth I said, "Carry her books."

"But you deserve that for what you did to her, *no*?"

I shrugged.

The kettle screeched. Señora Perez leaned into the metal table, got up, and turned off the hot plate. She brought over four mugs, a canister of loose tea, and a mesh tea ball.

Hannah asked, "How did you see Kelly carrying Charlotte's books?"

She stuffed the tea ball with leaves. "Does it surprise you that I go outside? I go around the neighborhood. Sometimes I chat with the neighborhood ladies."

Our eyebrows lifted a notch. "Really?" Darbie asked.

"Really," she said. "And I go to the store and the movies, and sometimes I make deliveries for special customers. Just yesterday, a lady who had an operation needed sea salt to soak her wound. Well, I have special sea salt from the Pacific Ocean. It is very good for healing. I brought it to her house."

I wondered if she was talking about Mrs. Silvers.

"I even went to your school to help organize in the library." She brought the kettle over and filled our mugs. She dangled the tea ball in Hannah's cup. The steamy water turned brown.

Darbie was determined to keep Señora Perez on the subject. "Why didn't you tell us about the Book the next time we saw you?"

"That was when you came in asking about the Law of Returns. You did not tell me where you learned about it. If you had said it was on a piece of paper in a book that looked like an encyclopedia, I would have known. But the idea of the Returns has been around for centuries among witches and even scientists."

Hannah asked, "You're saying that scientists believe in the Law of Returns?"

"There was a famous scientist who said 'to every action—"

"There is an equal and opposite reaction," Hannah interrupted. "That's Sir Isaac Newton."

"*Sí.*"

Hannah took the tea ball out of her mug and carefully swung it over to mine. She blew on her steaming liquid and took a sip. "Mmmm," she said.

"By the way, how did your good deeds work to reverse your bad luck?" Señora Perez asked.

"Mine did," Darbie said. "But, for the record, it sucked, pardon my French."

"If it was easy, it wouldn't have restored balance in nature."

Hannah completed the Señora's thought. "It wouldn't have had an equal reaction." She sipped her tea again. The reference to Newton seemed to have piqued Hannah's interest.

Señora Perez smiled at Hannah. "And what about you, *niña*? Did you do something good to stop the flying insects from stinging you?"

"I did something, but I don't think I'm finished. No more stings. But the mosquitoes have been eating me." She showed Señora Perez her arm.

Darbie and I glanced at each other because Hannah had been strange about keeping her good thing private. We used to share everything. We each had our own hot mug to stare into now that the tea ball had been dunked into everyone's water.

"What was your next clue that we had the Book?" I could practically see the invisible wall of tension between Hannah and us melt like a Swirley in a convection oven.

"I was quite positive when Kelly asked for vanilla bean from *Isla de Cedros*. Very few people know about the herbs from *Cedros*. The few people who come in here asking about Cedronian spices found information on the Internet computer."

Darbie tilted her head and narrowed her stare at Señora Perez. She pursed her lips and made a tough, serious face. "With the herbs from *Cedros*, people can make potions?"

"*Si*. People could."

Darbie said, "You could and you did. You wrote it down in the Secret Recipe Book." She would have made an excellent special guest star on a TV crime show.

"*Niñas*, let me tell you about the Book. It is a story that starts a long time ago. I came to the United States when I was about your age. We brought many spices from *Isla de Cedros*. My parents were farmers—they used the Cedronian herbs to bring good luck to their crop."

Hannah asked, "Did they grow the special herbs at their farm in Delaware?"

I wanted to smash into Hannah and give her a big bear hug because, finally, she believed this was all real. I smiled broadly. Darbie couldn't take her eyes off Hannah. It was like she couldn't believe that Hannah was finally with us on our quest for the truth.

Darbie leaned over and squeezed Hannah's cheeks between her hands until Hannah's lips were all smooshed together. "Welcome back," Darbie said. "I missed ya." She released Hannah's face and put her fist up for a bump. Hannah bumped it.

Señora Perez looked confused by this behavior.

"Sorry," Darbie said. "Tell us the rest of the story."

"You cannot grow the special herbs in Delaware because you need a shaman," she said.

"Yeah," Darbie said. "There's a shortage of them around here."

Señora Perez nodded and continued her story. "It was a very hot summer. I was twelve years old. I hadn't been in the U.S. very long, so I didn't have many friends. Usually, I worked at our farm stand. When I wasn't working, I went to the library. That's where I met two friends. One girl worked there filing books away. Another girl was a summer student studying chemistry. She wanted to be a doctor.

"One day they invited me to the pool. I was so happy to have friends. I told the girls about cooking. They didn't know much about cooking and wanted to learn. So they came over to my house and watched me make dinner for my family. They were amazed. For the next several weeks we cooked. I told them about the herbs from the *Isla de Cedros*. Immediately they wanted to experiment with the spices, which we did all summer. We kept a record of our recipes and the strange results. Some of the strange things were good and some not good.

"Then we noticed something happening to us. It was the Law of Returns. Whoever added the Cedronian spice to a recipe got bad luck. It took us many weeks to figure out the good deeds that would restore balance in the universe.

"One day we made a recipe to hex a boy we did not like. Each of us added some of the Cedronian spice so that the Return would be equally divided. The next day he was missing. I cannot tell you how we felt. It was terrible. We didn't mean to really hurt him.

"We did lots of good deeds to bring him back, but they were not enough. So we sacrificed something we loved. We stopped cooking. And a week later, he found his way home, but he could not see. We agreed that we must do a very difficult deed to create balance.

"We vowed not to make any more recipes. We pasted the pages of the Book into an old encyclopedia and put it away. School started a few days later. The science girl immersed herself in her studies. The library girl became involved in many school clubs and activities. Slowly, I made other friends. We three saw one another less each week. And slowly the boy regained a bit more of his eyesight. Eventually, when we three friends rarely saw one another, his eyesight came back completely.

"In our last conversation we decided the only way to put things right was for us to part as friends. And that is what we did."

"What about the Book?" Hannah asked.

"You see, the Book is what brought the three of us

together for a wonderful summer, and it was also the Book that broke us apart."

"That's so sad," Darbie said with tears in her eyes.

The room was quiet for a moment and we searched each other's faces, thinking about how we had nearly lost each other because of the Book—just like those girls did all those years ago. Then I saw through the small window above the sink that the sun had set and droplets of rain had begun to fall.

"What I don't understand," I said, "is that if you sell the Cedronian spices here, anyone can make potions."

"It is possible. Someone can buy my shade-grown ginseng and make a love potion if that is the intention in their heart when they're cooking. They may do it and not even realize it. They may be getting returns and not realize it. They may be undoing their returns with good deeds and not even know they are doing it."

"But people can also make hexes—the mean kind," I said.

"One herb can have many uses. I am certain that the spices I sell have more uses than I am aware of. I only know the ones that the girls and I used in our experiments. The sea salt from *Cedros* that I told you about earlier is a wonderful healer if it is boiled in water, but if it is baked on a ginger root . . . well, I'll just say it can be bad."

Hannah said, "Then maybe you shouldn't sell them."

"To do so would upset balance."

This comment caused another silence. I wondered if people were walking around Wilmington not realizing that they were under the power of some potion. And every time thunder cracked, did it mean someone was mixing a Cedronian herb into a recipe?

I asked, "So, how did the Book end up in my attic?"

"That is another mystery, I suppose." Señora Perez smiled.

I look at her with questioning eyes.

"*Chica*, you will have to figure that out on your own. On another day."

29

Two Weeks Later:
A Bet's a Bet

he gang's all here, as my dad says. But he wouldn't notice that Hannah wasn't there.

I did.

It was worse than I ever could have imagined. The entire neighborhood seemed to have come out to see the Barneys' new Japanese maple tree that Rusamano Landscaping had just planted. In front of Charlotte Barney's house stood Darbie; Frankie; Tony; Misty; Bud; Mrs. Silvers; Joanne; my dog, Rosey; and the Evil Maiden herself, Charlotte Barney.

When they saw me, they laughed.

And why wouldn't they? I asked myself.

There I was, wearing a frizzy, curly rainbow wig, a big red squishy nose, polka-dot pants, and a striped shirt, raking Charlotte Barney's yard in front of my friends and neighbors.

It might've been the worst day of my life—until I saw who was coming down the street carrying a huge Abercrombie & Fitch shopping bag. I didn't believe my eyes, but I could name that tune in two notes: *Freak Show*.

It was Hannah. She walked slowly so that she didn't trip over the flippers on her feet. She also wore a poodle skirt, Superman cape, cowgirl bandana, and sideways baseball cap.

She set the bag down on the sidewalk by the audience, picked up a rake, and came over to me.

"Abercrombie?" I asked, pointing at her outfit.

She nodded and raked. Charlotte and Misty died with laughter. I asked her, "Are you doing a good deed?"

"I decided the other day at practice, when Charlotte told me I should ditch you and Darbie as friends. She said you guys were holding me back from being totally cool and popular. I told her that I was trying to give her another chance to be a friend. But you were right, Kelly, she's just mean," Hannah said. "This?" She waved to her ridiculous outfit. "This is just an ordinary day hanging out with my BFF."

When I looked up to transfer my leaf pile into a trash

bag, I saw Tony holding a bag open for me. He had picked a tiara and lacy pink tutu from Hannah's bag. He helped me direct my leaves into the trash bag, flashing a mega-white smile meant only for me to see.

I smiled back.

Frankie was behind him. He was raking in a tall, striped *Cat-in-the-Hat* hat and bowtie. Darbie rummaged through the shopping bag in a way that reminded me of the day we cleaned out my attic. She found a black biker jacket and tap shoes. Bud slipped on a pair of fairy wings. He gave a flowery visor to Joanne.

They all got up to help me rake, except for Mrs. Silvers, who wasn't in any shape for yard work. But she did put on a colorful beanie hat with a propeller.

Even my mom came out of the house with a lampshade on her head, and Dad wore a paper bag with holes cut out for his eyes and mouth.

Suddenly, I realized we were all having fun.

Not Charlotte. She was still on the sidewalk with her arms crossed over her chest. When I first looked at her face, I thought she was angry. On a second look, I realized she was just sad.

Sam drove up in a new Sam's iScream On-the-Go truck and gave us all free Swirleys-To-Go. He said, "Looks like everyone is having a good time."

I said, "Just another day in Crazytown."

Here are a few recipes from the Book—and from Kelly, too!

Rocket Launching Rainbow Super Swirley

When you can't make up your mind, enjoy
this three-layered concoction.
Layer 1: Strawberry ice cream blended with colorful Skittles.
Layer 2: Banana ice cream with ribbons of golden caramel.
Layer 3: Bright green pistachio ice cream
peppered with Nerds candies.

Top with whipped cream and rainbow sprinkles.

Bowl Me Over Chocolate Brownie Super Swirley

Only for those able to handle the richest
possible combination of chocolate.
Chocolate fudge ice cream blended with chunks of brownie,
nibblets of semi-sweet chocolate morsels, hot fudge sauce, and
chunks of homemade Amish fudge. Snickers optional.
Swirl to perfection and top with a brick of rich brownie.

Black and White Super Swirley

Combines dark chocolate with creamy light vanilla.
Vanilla bean ice cream
Classic chocolate ice cream
Chocolate syrup

Blend until neither can be identified from the other.
Top with hot fudge.

Golden Buttercup Cakes

2 cups all-purpose flour
1½ cups sugar
2½ tsp baking powder
a pinch of salt
¾ cup butter or margarine (1½ sticks), softened
¾ cup whole milk
1½ tsp pure vanilla extract
2 large eggs

1. Preheat oven to 350°. Line 2½-inch muffin pan with cupcake holders.

2. Mix dry ingredients until combined. Add wet ingredients and beat just until blended and creamy.

3. Spoon batter into cups. Bake 20–25 minutes

Perfect Buttercream Frosting

1 pkg confectioners' sugar (16 oz)
½ cup butter or margarine (1 stick), softened
1½ tsp pure vanilla extract
2 tbsp cream

With hand mixer, beat sugar, softened butter, vanilla, and cream until blended. Increase speed until frosting is light and fluffy.

Love Bug Juice

(For l'amor)
4 cups cranberry juice
Fistful of maraschino cherries, mashed
2 slices kiwi fruit
1 diced apple
Dash of shade-grown Mexican ginseng

Mix all ingredients in a pitcher with lots of ice
and sprinkle generously with ginseng.

Keeps 'Em Quiet Cobbler

(Stopped the gallo from his early morning cockle—ip)
½ cup all-purpose flour
1 cup butter (2 sticks), softened
10 ripe apples, sliced
2 tbsp cinnamon
1 tsp ground cloves
2 tbsp almond paste
1 cup sugar
½ tsp aged vetivert stems

With a hand mixer, thoroughly beat flour, sugar, and softened
butter. Set aside. In separate bowl, mix apple slices with
cinnamon, cloves, almond paste, and vetivert stems. Add the
flour mixture and stir until well blended. Put into a baking
pan and bake uncovered at 350° for 45 minutes
or until apples are tender.

Hexberry *Tarta*

(Embrujar—*ip*)
2 pints berries
2 tbsp lemon juice
¼ cup all-purpose flour
½ cup sugar
½ tsp cinnamon
2 tbsp almond extract
2 tbsp unsalted butter
¼ cup shaved hazelnuts
Dash of rue seed
2 egg whites, optional
premade pie crust

*Mix all ingredients thoroughly and pour into pie crust.
If desired, brush the crust with egg whites. Bake at 350°
for 1 hour or until crust is brown and flakey.*

FCS: Fresh Citrus Squeeze

(For Causing Strife—ip)
Juice freshly squeezed from 3 oranges
1 tsp lemon juice
2 tbsp cherry juice
Mexican mint
Mix together and serve over ice.

Mrs. Rusamano's Annual Alfred Nobel Chili Cook-Off Award-Winning Chili

2 lbs lean ground beef

2 large green bell peppers, chopped

2 medium onions, chopped

2 stalks celery, chopped

4 tbsp minced garlic

2 fresh jalapeño chiles, chopped

1/3 cup chili powder

1 tsp cumin

1 14.5-oz can diced tomatoes

¼ tsp red peppers

2 bay leaves

1 15-oz can tomato sauce

6 cups water or beef broth

2 15.5-oz cans kidney beans

Salt to taste

Sauté meat, peppers, onions, celery, and garlic in a pan. Drain fat. Add everything except beans. Cover and simmer 1 hour, stirring occasionally. Add beans and simmer another 15 minutes.

Mrs. Quinn's Chili Recipe

1 lb ground beef or stew meat, browned and drained

1 medium onion, diced

1 small green pepper, diced

1 small red pepper, diced

1 can diced tomatoes

1 can chilis

1 can black beans
1 small can tomato paste
1 can dark beer
4 tbsp ground chili powder
2 tbsp cumin
1 tbsp nutmeg

*Brown beef, peppers, and onion. Drain off any grease.
Stir in the rest of the ingredients, adding the beans last. Bring to
a boil and reduce heat to low. Cover and cook on low for 1 hour.*

THE MAMMOTH

3 1-oz shots of espresso
16 oz brewed dark roast coffee
6 oz steamed milk

Whisk together.

ALFRED NOBEL SCHOOL CAFETERIA MASHED POTATOES

100 lbs potatoes, peeled, boiled, drained, and cut up
10 cups butter, softened
80 oz cream cheese, softened
80 oz sour cream

*Mix all of the above ingredients with an industrial mixer,
adding the butter and cream cheese in thirds.
Spoon and spread into 8½ x 13-inch glass dishes.
Bake until heated through.*

Tony's Favorite Tiramisu

2 cups heavy cream

½ cup plus 4 tbsp sugar

8 oz of mascarpone cheese

3 tbsp of crème de cocoa

1 cup strong coffee or espresso

20 ladyfingers or sponge cakes

⅛ cup of cocoa powder

serving dish

1. Whip 1 cup of the cream into stiff peaks, refrigerate while completing the next steps. Add 2 tbsp of sugar, or to taste.

2. In a separate bowl, whip the mascarpone cheese, ½ cup sugar, and 2 tbsp of crème de cocoa. Set aside.

3. Dip the top sides of half of the lady fingers in the coffee and place in the bottom of serving dish. You will need to cover the bottom of the dish, so only use as many ladyfingers as needed to do so.

4. Take refrigerated whipped cream and fold into the cheese mixture.

5. Spread one third mixture over ladyfingers and dust with cocoa powder.

6. Repeat steps 3 and 5, ending with the cheese mixture on top.

7. Take the reserved 1 cup of cream and 2 tbsp of sugar and whip till soft peaks are formed. Spread mixture over top of cheese layer and garnish with cocoa powder.

8. Chill tiramisu for at least 2 hours before serving!

Mrs. Rusamano's Cannoli

Shell:
1 cup flour

1 tsp baking powder

1 tbsp sugar

½ tsp cinnamon

1 tbsp butter

2 tbsp cold water

2 tbsp vinegar

Filling:
2 lbs ricotta cheese

1 tbsp vanilla extract

1½ cup sugar

½ cup chopped nuts

½ cup chocolate chips

½ cup citron (optional)

Shell:
Blend first four ingredients and add butter. Blend with your
fingertips as you would a pie crust. Add cold water and vinegar.
This makes a hard dough. Chill 1 hour.
Roll dough out to ½-inch thickness
and cut into 4 x 5-inch rectangles.
Roll dough around tubes, 1 inch in diameter.
Fry at 360° until brown. Drain and cool.

Filling:
Beat ricotta, vanilla, and sugar until smooth,
then add nuts, chocolate chips, and citron. Chill.
Fill crusts at both ends with filling.

Real life. Real you.

Don't miss any of these terrific Aladdin Mix books.

The Secret Identity of
Devon Delaney

Devon Delaney Should
Totally Know Better

Trading Faces

Portia's Exclusive and
Confidential Rules
on True Friendship

City Secrets

Home Sweet Drama

Ruby's Slippers

Nice and Mean

Things Are Gonna Get Ugly

Front Page Face-Off

Do you love the color pink?
All things sparkly? Mani/pedis?

These books are for you!

From Aladdin
Published by Simon & Schuster